Kids With Character

Kids With Character

*Preparing Children for
a Lifetime of Choices*

by
Marti Watson Garlett

MULTNOMAH

Portland, Oregon 97266

Unless otherwise marked, all Scripture references are from the Holy Bible: New International Version, copyright 1973, 1978, 1984 by the International Bible Society. Used by permission of Zondervan Bible Publishers.

Design by Paul Clark

KIDS WITH CHARACTER
© 1989 by Marti Garlett
Published by Multnomah Press
Portland, Oregon 97266

Multnomah Press is a ministry of Multnomah School of the Bible, 8435 N.E. Glisan Street, Portland, Oregon 97220

Printed in U.S.A.
Library of Congress Cataloging-in-Publication Data

89 90 91 92 93 94 95 96 97 98 - 10 9 8 7 6 5 4 3 2 1

An unlearned carpenter of my acquaintance
once said in my hearing,
"There is very little difference
between one man and another;
but what little there is, is very important."
This distinction seems to me
to go to the root of the matter.

William James

This book is affectionately dedicated to

David Koran

Theresa's husband
Jessica's father
my brother-in-law

a man with a difference

... There are two ways in which the human machine goes wrong. One is when human individuals drift apart from one another, or else collide with one another and do one another damage, by cheating or bullying. The other is when things go wrong inside the individual—when the different parts of him (his different faculties, and desires, and so on) either drift apart or interfere with one another. You can get the idea plain if you think of us as a fleet of ships sailing in formation. The voyage will be a success only, in the first place, if the ships do not collide and get in one another's way; and, secondly, if each ship is seaworthy and has her engines in good order. As a matter of fact, you cannot have either of these two things without the other. If the ships keep on having collisions, they will not remain seaworthy very long. On the other hand, if their steering gears are out of order, they will not be able to avoid collisions. Or, if you like, think of humanity as a band playing a tune. To get a good result, you need two things. Each player's individual instrument must be in tune and also each must come in at the right moment so as to combine with all the others.

But there is one thing we have not yet taken into account. We have not asked where the fleet is trying to get to, or what piece of music the band is trying to play. The instruments might be all in tune and might all come in at the right moment, but even so the performance might not be a success if they had been engaged to provide dance music and actually played nothing but Dead Marches. And however well the fleet sailed, its voyage would be a failure if it were meant to reach New York and actually arrived in Calcutta.

Morality, then, seems to be concerned with three things. Firstly, with fair play and harmony between individuals. Secondly, with what might be called tidying up or harmonizing the things inside each individual. Thirdly, with the general purpose of human life as a whole: what man was made for: what course the whole fleet ought to be on: what tune the conductor of the band wants it to play.

C. S. Lewis
Mere Christianity

CONTENTS

ACKNOWLEDGMENTS

Wouldest thou wit thy Lord's meaning in this thing?
Wit it well: Love was his meaning.
Who shewed it thee?
Love.
What shewed He thee?
Love.
Wherefore shewed it He?
for Love . . .
Thus was I learned that Love is our Lord's meaning.

Dame Juliana of Norwich

The following people have shown me particular love throughout the writing of this book and so to them I owe particular gratitude . . .

. . . Harold Fickett, Richard Foster, Howard Macy and all my fellow Fellows in The Milton Center—for encouragement, exhortation, and sustaining friendship.

. . . Liz Heaney, editor and teacher—for patience, perseverance, and incisive critique, as well as for steady belief in both this book and me.

. . . Madeleine L'Engle and Walter Wangerin—for timely reminders of story's central place in God's kingdom.

. . . Lynda Graybeal—for steering me toward a good word processing program I could actually afford.

. . . Gerardo Zuniga—for helping me extend my concept of family.

. . . my son Kyle—for never complaining, not even in the face of countless quickie meals.

. . . my son Marc—for generously allowing me to tell the story that wrote my last chapter for me.

. . . and, most of all, my husband Fred—for the cherished gift of strength and support. How much I've learned to lean on it! God bless you, darling.

A BEGINNING WORD

Good teachers, whether they're parents or professional educators, know something very important: They know they can't teach anyone anything. All they can do is make it possible for someone else to learn. All they can do is set the right conditions, create a receptive environment, establish an inviting tone.

I've been both a parent and a professional educator for over twenty years now. I've devoted nearly half my life to these twin roles and have discovered that they intertwine best under my parent's hat, not my teacher's.

Those of us who are parents must recognize early on that we're given primary responsibility for all the components that go into our children's education. We are our children's first, foremost, and most influential teachers.

It is our daily model, our daily leading, our daily living, that has the most impact on the students who "graduate" from our homes. Our children's education is within our parental power to control so long as we teach them to take control.

In other words, learning doesn't happen from the outside in. It happens from the inside out.

Or, in still other words, the task of all parents is to work themselves out of a job.

I hope this book will help you zero in on how to do that. The device I've chosen to use is God's own device of choice: *story.*

God is often revealed through action, through what

he does. Then we're told about it in story. Theologians call this "holy history."

Story is the closest those of us removed from the scene can come to experiential involvement in it. Story helps us enter into the moment, to experience it as if we were actually there, to live it and participate in it, to be an active part of it.

Furthermore, story figured prominently in Jesus' earthly ministry. He taught through story, over and over again. He made his teaching tangible through combining story and metaphor, parable and example. He fleshed out his meaning by using vivid illustration.

Story is not just entertainment, though that is certainly part of its attraction.

Story is necessity.

What you're holding in your hands is a collection of very human stories from very human teacher-parents. All these stories are real stories. Sometimes names have been changed, and sometimes I've taken liberties to combine certain events for purposes of clarity.

But in all instances the events underlying the stories are to-the-letter true. Every story in this book actually happened to people who—thank God!—share their common humanity with you and with me.

That means that what they've done is possible for all of us to do.

There's the key, right there. There's the heart and soul of this book—*seeing possibilities.*

Producing kids with character is not an impossible task. On the contrary, it's within the reach of every parent on the planet.

What liberation! What joy! Who among us can fail to draw strength and hope from recognizing what's possible?

I urge you to take from these stories whatever you need today, then read them again tomorrow and take from them whatever applies then.

To be sure, I haven't written anything resembling gospel. How could I? While I am writing prayerfully, that's not the same as putting Divine Truth in place. Even I am smart enough to recognize that.

I'm also smart enough to recognize that all families are unique. You and your children face challenges made up of nitty-gritty details I can't possibly know.

So what you must do is call upon God to help you fill in any gaps this book leaves. That is as it should be.

Ultimately, each of us must depend upon God and not a human educational authority, no matter how experienced he or she might be. God is our partner in seeing to our children's growth.

The task before me is to pull some good solid parenting principles from each of the stories I tell; the task before you is to forge a partnership with God.

It's God and not I who can help you cast a single beam of light in your life and focus it where it's most needed. It's God and not I who knows your deepest needs. It's God and not I who gave you the wonderful, maddening, challenging gift of those independent individuals you call your children.

My suggestion, then, is that you use this book as a guide for prayer and action, precisely in that order.

I

KIDS WITH CONFIDENCE

CHAPTER 1

"The Girl Who Feasted on Trinkets"

MARCY was a bundle of strong, sinewy, six-year-old energy. Quick to laugh, quick to cry, then quick to laugh again, Marcy's passion for living was intense and infectious. She kept her family in a state of animated flux.

Marcy's family lived on a dairy farm thirty miles or so from the nearest town. One of her delights was to ride into town with her mother and while her mother was next door buying groceries or down the block at the hardware store picking up supplies for her father, Marcy would spend her time slowly peering through all the bins of trinkets on display in the dime store.

The dime store fascinated Marcy. It was her babysitter. Content to be left on her own surrounded by colorful, accessible toys, Marcy would finger plastic dinosaurs and small trucks almost as if they were sacred icons.

She would hold up cardboard kaleidoscopes to the light and, twisting them, watch their geometric patterns change shape.

She would write her name sideways on a magic slate—M-A-R-C-Y, in bold block letters—and then, lifting the pages, make it disappear, a letter at a time.

The dime store proprietor was an old man everyone called Mr. Sam. He knew Marcy and her mother and would nod at them when her mother dropped Marcy off. Then he'd busy himself somewhere near the front counter, his tuneless whistle floating gently down the aisles.

One day Marcy saw that Mr. Sam had erected a new display. On it were packs of tiny playing cards which could easily fit into the palm of one of her hands. They were in boxes that looked like little bureau drawers. You pushed each "drawer" open and, presto, there they were: all sorts of impish animal faces grinning up at you.

Enthralled, Marcy had never seen anything so wondrous. She knew she couldn't leave this behind at Mr. Sam's store. No, this was something she had to have at home. How else could she take all the cards out individually and play with them?

So she just picked up one of the tiny boxes from its display case and shoved it down into the front pocket of her baggy corduroy jeans.

When her mother came to pick her up, Marcy waved good-bye to Mr. Sam and went out to the car for the return trip to the farm. She could feel the hard cardboard box rubbing against her leg as she walked, but she knew better than to touch it or pull it out or in any other way draw her mother's attention to the secret she carried.

Once home, she locked herself in the bathroom. Safe now, alone, she pulled out the cards and, squatting down, sorted them on the floor around her feet, neatly stacking all the matched partners together.

There were gray rabbits with pink noses, brown squirrels with bushy tails, spotted pigs with fat cheeks and merry smiles.

"What are you doing in there so long?" her sister called through the closed door. "Hurry up, Marce! I gotta go."

Melinda, at three years older, was a cross between a sometime playmate and a second mother.

Marcy froze at the sound of Melinda's voice. She blurted out, "Just a minute! I'm almost done."

Then she picked up the cards, shoved them back in their little cardboard drawer, and flushed the toilet. Finally, she opened the door, revealing Melinda's scowling face.

"You don't have to hog the bathroom, Marcy," Melinda said in irritation. "It doesn't belong just to you, you know."

Marcy ignored Melinda's pique. Instead she said, "Know what? Mother got me something at the store today."

"Mother got you something?" Melinda's eyebrows shot up. "Why didn't she get me something too?"

Marcy shrugged. "Maybe because you don't go to town with her very much."

"I don't believe Mother got you anything," Melinda said.

Marcy shrugged again, a great show of nonchalance. "Okay," she said, "suit yourself." She jiggled the box in her pocket.

Melinda's curiosity conquered her skepticism. "What is it?"

Marcy produced the small box of cards, holding it up to Melinda on the flat of her palm. "These," she said.

"What are they for?"

"They're for playing with, stupid. They're cards."

"Don't call me 'stupid.' I know they're cards. But Mother doesn't get us things for no reason, so why did she get you these? I want to know why."

Marcy was at a momentary loss. "Just because," she finally said.

"You're lying, Marcy."

"I am not!"

"Yes, you are. Mother didn't give you those cards, did she?"

"She did so!"

"She did not. You're lying. Mother! Mother, did you get Marcy a box of animal cards at the store today?"

So Melinda went off to find Mother and the jig was up. Marcy was caught in her lie—and in her thievery.

"Well, there's only one thing to do," Marcy's mother said decisively. "Take them back to Mr. Sam right now this very minute."

Marcy stood there, silent and quaking. As for Melinda, she casually but carefully placed herself behind their mother's shoulder where she could be sure that Marcy saw her. There was no denying her smug look of satisfaction.

Marcy and her mother went out to the car and, in virtual silence, drove the thirty-some miles back to town. They parked at one of the meters; Marcy was instructed to insert the nickel her mother handed her. Then, her hand firmly on Marcy's shoulder, Mother guided her daughter down the sidewalk, up the steps, and into the dime store.

Together they marched over to where Mr. Sam sat behind the cash register, whistling tunelessly.

"Mr. Sam," her mother said, "Marcy has something to tell you."

Marcy was pushed forward. Mr. Sam stopped his whistling and peered down. Marcy's knees barely held her upright.

She heard her mother's commanding voice. "Go ahead, Marcy. Tell Mr. Sam what you did."

Something rumbled in Marcy's throat. "I took these cards," she said.

Marcy was certain she had formed the words, but her mother said insistently, "What? No one can hear you Marcy. Go on now, tell Mr. Sam what you did."

So Marcy said louder, "I took these cards." Cautiously, as if they might break, she set them on the counter in front of Mr. Sam.

"You didn't pay for them, did you, Marcy?" her mother prodded.

"No." The "No" formed a big O across Marcy's mouth.

"And we don't take things we don't pay for, do we?"

"No." The O stayed where it was, unmoving.

"Tell Mr. Sam how sorry you are for taking something without paying for it."

Marcy sucked in a miserable breath. "I'm sorry," she said.

Mr. Sam's hand swallowed the animal cards Marcy had placed on the counter in front of him. He nodded curtly.

"Thank you," he said. His voice was gruff, though not unkind.

Somehow Marcy and her mother wound up back on the street in front of their car; Marcy had no memory of how they got there.

Away from Mr. Sam's eyes, Marcy's small, pointed chin started trembling and would not stop. Two tears spilled down cheeks already on fire with humiliation.

Wordlessly Marcy's mother took her little daughter into her arms and held her tightly. The floodgate of tears unlocked and Marcy sobbed.

Her mother held her until the tears and choking sobs subsided, then kissed her, smoothed her daughter's damp hair, and said, "I love you, Marcy. I love you very, very much."

Loving Unconditionally

When I finished telling this story to a friend of mine, he said, "You know, I think all of life is made up of us going to Mr. Sam with the cards we stole."

He may very well be right; I can't argue with him. I only hope that if all of life is made up of that, it's also made up of Marcy's mother taking us into her arms and saying, "I love you."

Actually, through the sacrifice of Jesus Christ, it is.

But our children won't know that unless we show them. It's our task as human parents to give our children at least a small glimpse of God's surpassing love.

The unconditional love of God is a gift, freely given. It's there because *we're* there.

Being loved unconditionally pierces to the very heart of self-confidence. If we don't receive unconditional love, we are unlikely to gain any confidence in ourselves. It frees us to accept ourselves and to forgive ourselves.

Marcy's mother required her daughter to live up to the law. Her love required that a wrong be righted. It demanded that her daughter strive for her best.

But Marcy's mother did not withdraw from her daughter. She did not cast Marcy out.

And so unconditional love was communicated to Marcy through unconditional support. Her mother stayed at Marcy's side.

But Marcy's mother did not attempt to chastise Marcy or heap guilt on her head. Returning the cards was punishment enough. The point had already been made.

Instead, Marcy's mother gave forgiveness. She gave *love.*

Humorist Erma Bombeck once wrote, "Children need our love the most when they deserve it the least." They need love when they lie to us, when they cheat and are unsportsmanlike, when they strike out in anger. They need love when they aren't chosen to be in the class play, when they lose the student election, when their grades bottom out, when they fail.

And, yes, let's say it: They need love when they come home drunk or stoned or pregnant. Our children need our love the most when they deny every value we've tried to instill in them.

Marcy's mother gave love to a small girl who desperately needed it. And in that moment Marcy's mother was the face of God.

Sadly, not all of us are as wise as this woman.

I was once asked by an acquaintance to help find a counselor for her thirteen-year-old daughter. Her daughter was uncontrollable, headed for trouble. The mother, rightly, was concerned.

Yet it was this same mother who—within my hearing and everyone else's at the grocery store—verbally upbraided her daughter for asking if she could spend the night at a friend's house.

"No, you can't spend the night! Why do you always bother me with stuff like that when I'm busy? I'm getting sick and tired of the way you ask for things whenever you feel like it, with no consideration for what I'm doing."

"But, Mom—"

"I told you, no! Are you having trouble with your ears, young lady? Is that just one more thing to add to the many that you're having trouble with?"

The mother's message was clear: "You make me sick and tired. If you want me to love you, then please be unnoticeable. Please slip into my life conveniently."

My embarrassment—and the other shoppers'—couldn't begin to compare with the daughter's. I'm sorry to say that this behavior was typical of this mother.

The daughter needed a friend, and I wanted to help her find one. I took the mother up on her request and recommended a wise and loving family counselor I know.

There's hope for this mother, and for all of us. It's not too late to change behavior and attitudes. God gave us an antidote—indeed, the only reliable antidote there is.

Love.

Growing up isn't as simple for children today as it was for me—and it wasn't all that simple for me. But at least when I grew up right and wrong were clearly defined. At least when I grew up the moral pathways were well marked.

Not so anymore. My children, and yours, have to contend with people who stick razor blades and poison in their Halloween candy. They have to contend with people who sell drugs on the playground, who take the shock out of violence by putting images of murder and mayhem on TV nightly, who bombard the media with persuasive messages like, "If it feels good, do it."

Our kids live in a tough, tough world. I don't know about you, but I've come to the conclusion there's not much I can do as a single individual to change the world my children live in. It's there, and it's cruel, and it's going to reach them before I can stop it.

All I can do is show love, directly and concretely. I can—exactly as you can—make every day a Valentine celebration.

We can write loving, encouraging notes and tuck them into our children's lunchboxes or sock drawers.

We can scrawl "I love you" in the steam on the bathroom mirror or tape it under the toilet-seat lid.

We can have messages printed in our newspaper's personal column, then clip them and hang them on our refrigerator.

We can occasionally, for no particular reason, serve dinner on the good china and pour our children's milk into the long-stemmed crystal. We can even lay a rose across their plates.

We can give our children our undivided attention when they talk to us. We can look directly into their eyes. We can put down our newspapers or knitting, turn off the television, ignore the telephone.

We can communicate respect for their ideas and feelings by making ourselves available to hear those ideas and feelings.

We can hug and kiss—*touch*—our kids every day. We can laugh with them, share jokes, enjoy them as people.

We can attend their events at school, support them with our presence and interest, write their activities on the calendar alongside our own.

Via word and deed, we can show our children that they occupy a place of importance in our daily lives.

We can greet our children warmly when they rise in the morning. We can sometimes have a glass of juice poured and waiting for them in the bathroom.

At night, we can personally tuck them in. Even when they're teenagers, we can kiss them as they rest on their pillows. We can sit on their beds and chat about the day's events (including the events of our day) and quietly say a prayer together.

Our children need to know that their presence in our daily lives is welcomed. We should communicate that we're glad to see them when they come home from school or when we pick them up after work.

At these critical end-of-the-work-and-school-day moments, there should be nothing more pressing on our agenda than being with our children. First, our children; second, our chores. In due time, we can prepare supper or go about our own evening tasks.

We can't expect our children automatically to know we love them. We have to tell them. Over and over, again and again. We have to tell them with words and show them with actions. Every single day.

Confidence in ourselves only comes when we feel good about ourselves. Believe me, children who know they're loved feel good about themselves.

And children who feel good about themselves are better able to handle any difficulty that life throws their way.

Questions for each of us to ask ourselves:
—Do my kids know I love them?
—Is one of my children easier to love? Do I show this? How can I display my love equally?
—What loving act can I do tomorrow that I didn't do today?

CHAPTER 2

"The Teacher Who Knew When to Laugh"

THE boy approaching Walt from down the hall was a slightly built fourteen-year-old wearing tight blue jeans and a black leather jacket, its collar arched near the narrow gold hoop threaded through his ear. His casual, confident attitude proclaimed, "I am in control; I fear no one; don't mess with me."

In contrast to the kid approaching him, Walt wasn't only modest in appearance, he was underwhelming. His shoulders drooped downward, as did his middle, and at the crown of his head was a mass of straight, dark hair that stubbornly resisted his efforts to keep it combed. It stuck out in several ridiculous-looking directions.

Walt knew, via the faculty grapevine, one important fact about the boy approaching him. He knew that this kid was a Discipline Problem, one tough independent cookie who was not only willing but anxious to frustrate even the best-hearted efforts of good teachers.

On this particular morning, Walt was standing against the wall near the doorway to his classroom. And on this particular morning, Walt had a typical teacher malady.

He had a headache.

In one of his hands was an aspirin. In his other hand was a mug lettered with the words I ARE A ENGLISH TEACHER. Inside the mug was a congealing mixture of cold coffee and undissolved Cremora. Walt's intent was to pop the aspirin into his mouth and wash it down as quickly as possible.

Meanwhile, the boy strutted nearer. His quick eyes grazed Walt's, in one glance, taking in the aspirin and the mug. A private smile slid across his face.

His lips barely moved but his words were clear and audible. "Birth control pill, I hope," he said.

Walt had no trouble hearing the comment. The boy made sure of that.

Now Walt had a decision to make. As he saw it, he could deal with the kid in one of three ways. He could grab the smart aleck by the collar and haul him down to the principal's office. Maybe that would wipe the grin off his face and teach him a little respect.

Walt knew this was what the kid was expecting. In fact, he was almost daring Walt to do it.

Walt didn't know him, but Walt suspected the kid's insolence was getting worse, not better. That was the pattern for most Discipline Problems fed with a regular diet of principal's office.

So Walt considered a second option—ignoring the comment and the kid, looking through and past him as if he didn't exist.

Junior high teachers learn early that Discipline Problems detest going unnoticed by authority figures. Being noticed is their reason for being.

In Walt's opinion, ignoring a kid, even a Discipline Problem, was at best spiteful, at worst vengeful. And Walt wasn't comfortable with the idea of teachers wreaking vengeance on their students. So out went option two.

Anyway, Walt didn't like shutting his eyes to things. He liked to give what was in front of him clear-eyed scrutiny. How else could you see what needed fixing?

That left only one more option. Laughing out loud. What, after all, was so offensive about the comment? Actually, Walt thought it was pretty funny.

Doggone it, if the kid had wit, the kid had humor. And if the kid had humor, then the kid didn't take himself too seriously. And if the kid didn't take himself too seriously, maybe he was an all right kid, a healthy kid.

It was the humorless kids—the humorless *human beings*—who worried Walt. Now *they* were trouble. *Big* trouble.

Options one and two disappeared; Walt responded with option three—he laughed.

Loudly and appreciatively.

No doubt about it, Walt's laughter was genuine. And so flashed a moment of rapport between Walt and one of this junior high's main Discipline Problems.

The kid threw Walt an interested look. Who are you? the look seemed to ask. Some sort of real guy or something? You got a sense of humor or something? What gives, man? Aren't you a teacher?

Meanwhile, Walt was nodding amiably, almost as if he understood every one of the unspoken questions.

"Yeah, birth control pill," Walt finally replied, looking down at the white tablet in his hand. "But, hey, what can I do? It's doctor's orders."

He made a show of placing the aspirin on his tongue. "He told me, my doctor did, he said, 'Walt, how many times do I hafta tell you? You gotta take your pills. Doncha know there're too many of you in the world already?'"

The boy's swagger slowed, and for an instant he looked like a normal adolescent male.

"Too many of you?" the kid said. "Maybe there

are"—now his eyes met Walt's directly—"and then again, maybe there aren't."

Developing Humor

As a teenager I read a lot of magazine advice columns about what to look for in a future mate. "Sense of humor" was *always* at the top. I wondered how I was supposed to recognize a sense of humor when I saw it. The first thing I centered on (I was probably fourteen at the time) was the obvious: I'd look for someone who could tell good jokes.

Well, it didn't take long for me to learn that knowing jokes to tell and how to tell them does not a sense of humor make.

I learned a sense of humor stems from perspective. I learned that the people I was most attracted to were able to keep from taking too seriously the events of their daily lives. In particular, they were able to keep from taking *themselves* too seriously.

Walt knew this, so instead of himself, he took the boy seriously. What did he do that was so important? He treated a troubled teen like he would any normal human being—any friend, for that matter. Walt joked with him. That was all.

Simple, yet extraordinary!

When I first heard Walt tell this story, I was sitting in an audience of teachers and school administrators. We laughed when he told the part where the kid made the comment, "Birth control pill, I hope."

That wasn't unusual, of course. What was unusual was that Walt laughed when it happened. Most of us probably wouldn't have. Most of us would have reserved our laughter for later, when we told the incident to someone else.

How many of us, faced with that kid's comment, would have been self-consciously, maybe even self-righteously, *adult?* How many of us would have squelched our spirit of playfulness until later when it was more safe, more acceptable?

Thank God for those like Walt who don't squelch it, for those who invite kids to interact with them on a playful level.

Actually, a humorous tone pervades the classrooms and homes of many teachers and parents I know.

One teacher throws erasers and trash cans to get students' attention. He writes goofy comments on their tests. He wears loud Hawaiian shirts, often the same one several days in a row.

Another teacher has her students memorize Shel Silverstein rhymes and then gives silly awards for the most outlandish, outrageous recitations.

A parent tucks "The Far Side" cartoons into her kids' clean laundry or between the pages of their textbooks.

Another parent brings home a video retrospective of several Monty Python movies, then pops popcorn and settles in for a weekend of celebrating laughter with his family.

Another family plays dictionary together. They sort through the dictionary to find a word no one knows, then hide that word's real definition in among each family member's own concocted definition.

Long-running gags are fun ways to share closeness, to bind us to each other, to develop our ability to laugh at ourselves. When Fred and I were married in 1965, my sister Luree gave us a gift tied up with a beautiful two-tone blue silk bow. That Christmas I returned the bow to her on her gift. The next Christmas she had the bow concealed *inside* our gift.

And so it has gone, changing hands every year. Everyone enters into the planning of where and how the blue bow will next surface. At various times, the infamous blue bow has been canned, made into a jigsaw puzzle, photographed indelibly on an apron, sent by proxy from another state, appeared mysteriously on the back of a painting already hanging in the "victim's" house—and on and on and on. It has become the most sorry-looking blue silk bow you've ever seen.

When Luree got married, our children helped us remove all the identifying labels from the canned goods in her kitchen.

Such playfulness is catching.

Once when I had a magnetic pad of paper on my refrigerator that had two little pigs standing in the corner of each page, Marc penciled in a spray of water from one pig's mouth so that it would shower the other pig. The pig being showered then calmly produced a long-handled brush and began scrubbing his back.

But you couldn't see this all at once. Only by flipping the sheets of paper rapidly could you get the whole effect. Marc's creation was a moving picture. My son had left an animated cartoon on my refrigerator for me!

Our family is notorious for tickling matches, for trying to sneak up and overpower each other. Nowadays my sons usually win. In fact, they usually throw me over their shoulder. I have a chipped front tooth, courtesy of some spirited wrestling with an adult-sized "child"!

In the course of my professional life, I travel frequently. I try to bring something fun home to my children. One time I brought Kyle a pillowcase that said, "You don't have to brush all your teeth, Kyle, only the ones you want to keep." Humorous gifts can protect kids from tiresome lectures and still get our point across.

When I was teaching in Korea—far, far away from home—Marc sent me a tape to help combat my homesickness. The first side of the tape took me on a light-hearted tour of our house.

"I know you're lonely, Mom," said his familiar voice, coming across several thousand miles, "so I'm going to bring you home for a little while. Here I am in the living room; there, I've just put your grandmother's rocking chair into motion. Can you see it?

"Now here's a run down the piano [I could hear him drag his hand across the keys]. Oops, that brought Cricket awake. Say hello to Mom, Cricket. Now I'm headed through the front hall and up the stairs.

"Okay, you're climbing the stairs with me. I think I can hear Kyle up in the den, messing with the computer. Sure enough, there he is. Say hello to Mom, Kyle."

And so forth. I was delighted—as Marc knew I would be. I sent one back in kind.

Conveying our own humor, as well as enjoying theirs, sends a reassuring, hope-giving message to our children through the God-granted gift of laughter.

During a recent faculty meeting—that is, during a recent, particularly *boring* faculty meeting—a religion professor friend of mine sitting next to me took my pad of paper and wrote, "Ho-hum. How about a contest? Who has the crummiest-looking shoes?"

I wrote down my reply—a toss-up between two fellow faculty members sitting across from us.

Next, my thoughtful theologian colleague wrote: "Sharpest shirt?"

I wrote down the name of the person who got my vote.

Then it was my turn to ask a question. "Who," I wrote, "is doing the best 'I'm listening' acting job?"

He thought a moment, then wrote down his choice. When I glanced at the person he'd named—a person molded perfectly into Rodin's famous *Thinker* pose—it nearly cracked us both up. We had to look away from each other to stifle our laughter.

I came home that evening and told Kyle how I had amused myself during a dull, dry, pointless faculty meeting, and he said, "Mom, you're no better than us kids—and *you're* in your forties!"

I took it as a great compliment.

I've learned that if we like our children, we'll laugh with them. It will come naturally.

Humor allows us to look at life with a twinkle in our eye. It's what allows us to pull joy from the moment, to release natural chemicals into our bloodstream that flood us with well-being.

Humor keeps any one thing from becoming too important to us, including ourselves. That's why people who have the proverbial "good sense of humor" are so likable. They put a healthy, light-hearted perspective on people and events—indeed, on all of life.

Each of us is a human being, and humor reminds us of that fact. It restores sanity and balance to our territorial kingdoms. "It's not only perfectly all right to be human," humor tells our children, "it's the only thing any of us is expected to be."

And so from humor kindness grows. With humor, the peculiarity or particularity of another need not threaten us. Knowing how and when to laugh at ourselves releases us to accept uniqueness in others. Boundaries fall.

In other words, humor frees. It frees us, and it frees those who interact with us.

Our kids need the freedom that humor brings.

Questions for each of us to ask ourselves:
—Do my kids take themselves too seriously? Do I?
—On a scale of 1 to 10 (1 being low, 10 being high), what is the part playfulness and laughter play in my home?
—What can I do to make laughter a more important part of my family's time together?

CHAPTER 3

"The Girl Who Stored Up Birthdays"

Laurel was four years old the Christmas that one of her family's most important traditions began. It began because of Laurel.

"If it's Jesus' birthday," she asked her mother one day shortly before Christmas, "how come we don't have a birthday cake for him?"

Laurel's mother Doris would always remember hugging her small daughter and saying firmly (though she had just made up her mind to do it), "We will! Yes, we'll have it on Christmas Eve before Santa comes. In fact, we'll make a great big party of it!"

On the Christmas Eve that this tradition began, Doris rose early to bake a tall angel food cake. What could be more appropriate for Jesus' birthday than angel food cake?

It had to be a special birthday party—one that centered on Jesus and not on all the gifts Santa was bringing. Everyone in the family loved picnics, so why not have a picnic? A cookout and picnic in the middle of winter couldn't help but make it special.

Doris decided the complete birthday menu would be hamburgers and the sort of relishes and side dishes that went along with a summer cookout: deviled eggs, baked beans, pickles, tomato slices, lettuce, green onions, potato chips.

For a distinctive holiday touch, egg nog was added. And of course angel food cake with flaming candles would provide the fitting birthday conclusion.

The prettiest place to have Jesus' birthday party was on the floor beside their brightly lit Christmas tree. Besides, the tree made it seem like a party was already in progress.

Doris spread a tablecloth on the floor by the tree and laid out paper plates and napkins. A picnic needed to be a picnic.

When the cake was presented, the family burst spontaneously into the traditional birthday song, automatically personalizing the words for their honored Birthday Guest:

Happy birthday to you,

Happy birthday to you,

Happy birthday, dear Jesus,

Happy birthday to you!

Laurel clapped her hands with joy and blew out Jesus' candles.

Thus began a treasured tradition that even the children who came after Laurel—*her* children—would celebrate with the same sense of wonder and thrill.

As for those years when there were no children, when everyone in attendance was an adult, well, the family still had their ritual picnic on the floor by the Christmas tree.

How could they not? It was *tradition.*

"Sunday night supper" was another favorite tradition. This came to be a time reserved each week for eating a special meal together and playing games. Nothing was allowed to intrude on these times of focusing on each other.

The menu was as traditional as any other part of the ritual: salami and cheese and fresh seasonal fruit.

The nibble-as-you-go meal was served buffet style and then carried to the "gaming room" on bamboo lap trays. It could last—and usually did—for hours.

And while it lasted, everyone played games, sometimes card games, sometimes board games. The most popular game of all was reserved for those special times when grandparents or aunts and uncles and cousins came visiting. Then the paper and pencils were brought out *en masse*, marking the beginning of a round of charades.

As everyone grew older and got married, the in-laws would say that charades was a rite of passage they'd had to pass through in order to be accepted into the family.

If you weren't adept at pantomime (so the family folklore went), if you were the least bit shy about making a fool of yourself in front of your date's family—well, sorry, Jack, but don't even consider marrying our daughter!

So games and ritual meals became part of a precious, shared family history. Whatever else befell them, this was something they held in common.

It marked them "indivisible."

Indeed, the indivisibility forged in playing games together went back at least four generations.

Laurel's grandparents, parents, Laurel and her brothers and sisters, and eventually *their* children all played charades together in exactly the same way, with exactly the same spirit of joy and adventure. Even though Laurel's grandparents died before her children were born, there was kindredness in knowing they had all shared a passion for charades.

This pervasive constancy in their lives helped Laurel and her siblings know they belonged to something larger than themselves. It helped them see that they were part of something strong and enduring, that there were familiar faces in this world who cared about them and to whom they could turn and share tears or triumphs or a few hours of good conversation. Tradition knit their family together.

Bonding to Family

Memories imprint people for a lifetime. It's the ritual of doing things again and again that gives memories their "forever" quality. And it's *never* too late to start a family tradition. They all began somewhere at the initiation of someone.

Often children's first glimmer of God is found in common, ordinary rituals: bedtime prayers, saying grace before meals, attending church. When we regularly pray and worship, when we demonstrate how important prayer and worship are in *our* lives, they are more likely to become important in our children's lives too.

Being raised in a Christian home is not a substitute for personal responsibility, of course. Each of us must choose individually whether or not to follow God. But knowing that they belong to a "host of witnesses"—to Christian parents and grandparents and uncles and aunts—helps shape children's future choices. It gives them an advantage, a head start.

All of us are influenced by our family connections. We all discover part of who and what we are through the people who claim us as theirs.

In his book *Who Switched the Price Tags?*, sociologist Tony Campolo offers this bit of sage advice:

> When parents ask me how they can help their children to overcome insecurities, I answer, "Ritual!" When parents ask me how they can get their children to embrace the right kind of behavior patterns, I say, "Ritual!" When parents ask how they can give their children good feelings about themselves, I say, "Ritual!"
>
> Tevye was right. Without ritual, children forget what they should remember and lose sight of what they should believe. Without traditions, children fail to learn how to behave. Without

ritual, they become as shaky 'as . . . as . . . as . . . a fiddler on a roof.'

A strong sense of family helps satisfy our children's need to see themselves as part of a larger picture. Where there's strong identity with people, there's a strong identity with the values those people hold.

My father is a man of integrity. He's a man of few words, unshowy. Unafraid of hard work, he's a longtime political activist who believes in citizen responsibility, who takes the democratic process and his role in it very seriously.

My mother, on the other hand, is boisterous, at times volatile. She's also fun-loving, warm, and sensitive, a woman devoted to her family who's unafraid to take risks, a woman eager to court adventure. She reads constantly, is intrigued by ideas, exults in good conversation.

In many ways I'm different from either of my parents, yet there also are—undeniably—basic similarities. I'm loyal and patriotic. Furthermore, I read avidly, am passionate about ideas, enjoy lively debates.

I also delight in laughter and play. "Fun" is perhaps my all-time favorite word; at least, I'm always ready for it. I'm not only willing to take risks, I seek them.

And when I love, I love ferociously.

How did I acquire these values?

Yes, I saw them constantly modeled, constantly lived out in my childhood home.

However—and this is *very* important—I believe there was something even more crucial to the development of my individual values. I believe my parents gave me *such a strong feeling of family identity that whatever they were, I wanted to be too.*

For years and years—in truth, for more years than we can count—the Watson side of my family has gathered for an annual reunion. It's a multi-generational affair. When everyone is there, the family count hovers around sixty.

Together we celebrate marriages and births, mourn deaths and divorces—a supportive network of arms reaching across miles and years, spanning generations.

Being one with my family was how I rooted myself in a big, alien world. I was shaped by my family's traditions. Because there were things about my family I knew I could count on, traditional things that *always* happened, I was able, as a child, to find security.

It's been said children need two things to be whole: They need roots, and they need wings. Roots provide them with their foundation; wings carry them on their way.

Alex Haley recorded his family's history in *Roots*, a novel celebrating genealogy. Degraded by slavery, the family in Haley's book eventually learns pride in its heritage by discovering kinship to a noble African prince.

Focusing on family history is a good gift for Christmas or some other important family event (say, a fiftieth wedding anniversary or the birth of a first grandchild). My friend Liz put together an album that reflected her family's history.

The album Liz compiled included facts about her grandparents and parents—places they'd lived, education they'd received, jobs they'd held. She included a family tree, and her parents' personal reflections about World War II. She also, of course, included family photographs, as well as copies of such memorabilia as grade cards, awards, and honeymoon receipts.

Albums filled with family history provide an enduring legacy for generations to come.

Traditions aren't always serious; they can be playful. I have heard of two brothers who are even more outrageous than my sister and I are with our blue bow tradition.

Howard gave Harold a pair of expensive cashmere pants for his birthday. The only trouble was, the pants were a hideous color. Harold had no desire to keep the pants, much less wear them. So on Howard's birthday,

Harold sent the pants back. Actually, he had them dropped from an airplane over Howard's house.

Well, Howard didn't much want to keep or wear the hideous cashmere pants either. On Harold's birthday, Howard bought an old car at a junkyard, put the pants inside, had the car squashed into a tidy rectangle of mashed steel, and made certain it was delivered to Harold's driveway.

Now it was Harold's turn again. This time the pants were covered with wet concrete. When everything hardened into a slab, Harold hired a dump truck to pitch it onto Howard's lawn.

And so it goes between Howard and Harold. They are having, I think it's fair to say, tremendous fun carrying on this wacky— if expensive!—family tradition.

Family ritual doesn't wear any one face. It's not just special events or gifts. It can come in many different guises.

In some families it's traditional for everyone to learn to play the violin.

In others it's traditional on Memorial Day to plant flowers at the headstones of loved ones' graves.

In still other families what's traditional is limping down the aisle on your wedding day with Grandma's lucky gold sovereign in your shoe.

A New Year's Day tradition the Felix family instituted includes serving a pot of black-eyed peas for dinner. A dime is stirred into the pot.

The adventure, of course, comes in seeing who will be served the hidden dime. Guests are always included in the family fun. Whoever discovers the dime on his or her dinner plate is supposed to have an especially good year. It's also, I'm told, an excellent way to get children to eat their vegetables!

But no matter what form rituals may take, bonding to family is the common thread uniting them all. Bonding to family breathes security into a child's life.

My children and yours, through emphasis on family tradition, can develop strong roots which give rise to wings. They can be carried aloft all their lives. We hold the power within our homes, within our families, to infuse our children with a lasting spirit—the spirit of self-confidence.

It's a paradox, isn't it? A sweet, healthy paradox: Bonding them to us can set our children free.

Questions for each of us to ask ourselves:

—Did my family have traditions? What were they? Am I passing them on to my children?

—What are some family traditions I could begin implementing right now?

—What is distinctive about our family? Who are we? When my children think about our family, what image will come to mind?

CHAPTER 4

"The Dad Who Had to Eat Lunch"

ED, the father of two, was a fairly typical dad. He went to work everyday, got home just in time for supper, took a computer class on Tuesday and Thursday nights, mowed his lawn on Saturdays, ushered in his church on Sundays. His time with his children was limited.

Not unlike many fathers, he wished he could see more of them. He wanted to know them better, to know them *well*, not just interact with them on a surface level.

Ed began to think about who it was in his life that he knew fairly well—who were his friends and what made them his friends?

The more he thought about it, the more he realized that the people he knew best were the business colleagues he ate lunch with. There seemed to be something personal and dynamic, perhaps even intimate, about eating lunch together.

Was this the key? Eating lunch together?

Ed decided to test this possibility on his son and daughter, and so he set aside one lunchtime a week for each child.

He called their two school principals—Mike was in junior high, Jamie in elementary school. The plan was to take Mike out for lunch every Tuesday and to take Jamie out every Thursday. Those were the evenings Ed was gone from home, the nights he felt more frustrated than usual at not having enough time with his kids.

Since Mike's lunch period was short, Ed would take Mike someplace near the junior high. On nice days they'd order from McDonald's drive-through window and take their bag of burgers over to the 4-H building's quiet parking lot. Then they'd sit on the hood of the car and eat and talk.

"So how's your day going, Mike?"

"I dunno, Dad. Not that great. I don't think my P.E. teacher likes me."

"What's not to like?" asked Mike's father indignantly. "Tell me what the problem is."

A shrug from Mike. "He's always on my case."

"In what way?"

"Oh, I dunno. Like telling me to run faster, to put on more speed, you know, to kick butt. Stuff like that."

Ed knew better than to comment on Mike's word choice; he wanted nothing to interfere with his son opening up and talking to him. "Does he think you're not trying hard enough?" Ed asked.

Another shrug. "I guess."

"So what do you think?"

"Jeez, Dad, I'm just not a fast runner. I'm so dang slow. I *want* to run faster, I want to keep up with the other guys. But I can't. Like, for instance, I'm always the last one in the class to finish laps."

"Yeah, I know how that feels," Ed said. "That's pretty much the way I was too."

"You were?"

"Yeah. I remember one time when I went out for football, we had to do these things called 'pursuit drills.' "

"What's a pursuit drill?"

"Well, it's where one guy runs down the field and five other guys chase him and try to tag him. Whoever can't put the tag on him has to drop for push-ups."

"So did you catch him?"

"Never. Not even once. I did lots of push-ups, and I gotta tell you, I hated it."

Mike was interested. "What'd you do about it?" he asked.

"There wasn't much I could do except practice running on my toes more. I used to run pretty flat-footed. Running on my toes helped some, but mostly I had to develop my athletic abilities in areas that didn't require running—like golf and swimming and wrestling." Ed grinned. "And hey, you know what? I got pretty good at those things!"

"You did?"

"Yeah," Ed said, "and the guys who could run fast finally learned I wasn't geeky because I couldn't. They learned, like I did, that while there were some things I couldn't do as well as they did, there were other things I could do better." Ed tossed down a few French fries. "We all just had to find out what our own individual talents were, that's all."

Father and son chewed in companionable silence for a minute, then Ed added, "Look, Mike, I hope your P.E. teacher is the kind of teacher who'll help you discover the things you can be really good at. I hope he'll help you develop in those areas. But if he doesn't, I will. So let me know how it goes, okay?"

"Sure, Dad, okay."

Unlike her brother, Jamie had a whole hour for lunch. The extra time allowed Ed to drive her across town to a favorite cafe near where he worked.

"I hate Mrs. Lynch," Jamie said one day soon after plopping onto the car's front seat. "She always yells at me."

Ed shot his eleven-year-old a quizzical glance. "She yells at you? I'll bet that doesn't feel too good."

"You got that right," Jamie responded. "Like today, for instance. Everyone in the whole class heard her yelling at me. Probably everyone in the whole school heard her."

"What did she yell at you about?"

"She yelled because I didn't put my name on my paper. She says I'm always not putting my name on my paper."

"Oh? Do you just forget to write it, or what?"

"Yeah, I forget to write it sometimes. So big deal. Everybody forgets sometimes. Boy, I hate that lady!"

Ed slowed for a traffic light. "What did you do when Mrs. Lynch yelled at you?" he asked. "Did you yell back?"

"I wanted to."

"I'll bet you did. I know I sometimes want to yell at someone when I get really embarrassed."

"Yeah, but see, I didn't do it, Dad. I didn't yell back. I just went up and got my paper like she told me to, and then I put my name on it."

The light changed to green, and Ed moved the car forward, this time his glance toward Jamie holding a smile. "I'm proud of you, honey," he said. "You handled that in exactly the right way."

Feeling Important

Ed sent a strong and vital message to his two children: They were important to him.

In his feelings for his children, Ed wasn't any different from the rest of us. Your children are important to you, and mine are important to me.

What Ed did differently than perhaps what most of us do was to let his kids *know* how important they were to him.

All children need to hear this message from their parents. More than hearing it, they need to see it. Mike and Jamie had no trouble seeing it. Every week their dad took them out to lunch—an investment of his personal time, and they knew it. No one else's dad picked them up weekly and treated them to lunch.

Because of this special treatment, they knew their dad liked them. They knew he wanted to be with them. He went out of his way to show them. This simple act caused Mike and Jamie to see their own worth and value. They felt enjoyed as human beings.

They felt important.

We don't have to take our kids to lunch to reach the same end. Some parents set aside a particular evening or a particular Saturday for scheduling outings with their children.

I know a mother who regularly takes her children to movies. Often she sees the same movie several times simply because she knows that while it's the kind of movie all her children would enjoy, they would each enjoy it more if they were with her alone. And the movie feels new to her each time; she sees it through the eyes of whichever child she's with. Their enjoyment is her enjoyment.

Sheryl's son, Keith, loves baseball. Someday he would like to play it on the college level. At great financial sacrifice, Sheryl bought Keith a pitching machine for his fifteenth birthday. She makes time each week to go to the park with him. Sheryl feeds balls into the machine while Keith practices his batting.

Jerry and his son, Steve, discovered the joy of cycling. They worked on conditioning and endurance together, and now they take hundred-mile-plus bicycle trips all over the place, just the two of them.

When we let our children know they can count on spending special time with us, we provide built-in security, a built-in sense of specialness.

During the eight years I produced KAKE-TV's "Romper Room" the truth of this came home to me through our favorite friend, Do Bee. I saw children's love of routine, of being able to count on special moments.

Every Monday and Friday morning, Do Bee visited us. The children couldn't wait. Even the shyest of them would throw their arms around Do Bee, secure in the knowledge that he was there simply to hug them back. Through routine contact, Do Bee helped children know they were important.

The type of outing isn't important. What *is* important is that we deliberately allow each one of our children to bask occasionally in our full attention, that they not always be required to share us with another sibling or, for that matter, with our spouse.

When we spend time with our kids, we discover their thoughts and dreams, what makes them laugh and what brings them joy, what triggers their anger and their sorrow.

And when guidance is needed, we must guide tenderly and without judgment—precisely as Ed did. Whatever feelings Ed's kids expressed to him, he accepted because he knew feelings are neither right nor wrong.

When we accept our kids' feelings, we demonstrate our respect for them; we recognize them as people. That makes them feel important. I believe it also helps them learn that all people, even the least among us, are worthy of respect.

We can show respect for kids' feelings by *not* saying, "You shouldn't feel that way." When *we're* frustrated, aren't we likely to react with anger? I know I am.

Nothing's wrong with feeling angry. How I choose to act on that feeling could be wrong, certainly. But no one helps me or shows me respect when he says, "You really shouldn't feel that way." Just as unfortunate is the pious question, "Now what do you think God is trying to teach you?" When our children open up and share their feelings with us, we can demonstrate our respect for them by not lapsing into pat responses or rote platitudes.

Another way we can show respect is to acknowledge our children's need for privacy. We should knock on their bedroom doors and wait to be invited in before we enter. Their rooms are their sanctuaries. They need those sanctuaries. We all do.

We show respect for our children by opening our homes to their friends. Warm and gracious hospitality says, "I trust you and the choices you make. Besides, I like your friends too. I hope you know they're welcome in this house anytime."

We also show respect for our children by being their biggest fans. I have attended many a school football or church league basketball game, many a debate or fencing tournament (even when I had to drive across state lines to get there), many a concert or music contest. To endure alone the stress of competition is very, very difficult. To have no one to cheer with you when you win is even worse.

My college students tell me of a great many things that their parents did to make them feel special. What follows are some of their recollections.

Lichelle: "I could talk very comfortably about any and everything to my parents, *anytime.* That helped because I did not have the pressure of keeping things inside or feeling like I could not go to my parents."

Tara: "When I was in junior high, my mother quit her job in order to stay at home to support and encourage me during the hectic years of adolescence. It made me feel special to know that my mom put me ahead of her own desires."

Kelly: "The one thing my parents did and still do is tell me how much they love me."

Earnie: "Once when I was in the fifth grade my parents went to school to talk to the principal about a punishment we felt was unfair to me. It made me feel really good, not to mention loved, to know that they would stick behind me like that."

Julie: "When we were little, my mom used to tape record my twin sister and me reading and singing. She'd play those tapes a lot, even when relatives and friends came over."

Shelley: "Sometimes my mom would take my brother and me to work with her. She felt we were important apart from home, so important that she'd even bring us into her professional world.''

Debrah: "My tough dad's tenderness made me feel important. He taught me to tie my shoes. I was four and it was just the two of us—me on his lap, secure, warm, totally involved. He also taught me to drive with the same patience and attentiveness—just he and I and the old car headed down a long country road."

These simple yet precious memories will stay with these students forever.

We must never become so busy that we don't take time to notice what's important to our kids. More to the point, kids need to see us noticing.

Please don't misunderstand. When I say it's essential to show our children how important they are to us, I'm *not* talking about instilling them with arrogance or an inflated sense of their own worth. Far from it.

What I'm talking about is giving our children the gift of themselves. I'm talking about allowing them to be comfortable with who they are, to grow up whole and secure.

When our children are secure in their importance to us we give them the inner strength to reach beyond themselves, to rise above obstacles, to tap unknown reservoirs, to seek adventure and risk undertaking what is new and untried. This sense of significance allows our children to be different, to be their own persons, to stand resolute against evil, to hold firm and fast against the fearsome winds of a worrisome world.

A mother once told me she refused to praise her children to their faces or in any way make them feel that she was proud of them for fear they'd become big-headed. No way did she want spoiled, self-important kids on her hands, she said.

Well, she certainly spared herself that. Her children were neither spoiled nor self-important.

What they were was timid, insecure, and fearful. They interpreted her silence as disapproval, even dislike. They interpreted it as indifference.

The opposite of feeling important is not some sort of biblical humility.

No, the opposite of feeling important is feeling *un*important.

During their adolescence, this woman's children declared open war on her. They liberated themselves from her beliefs and attitudes through teenage rebellion. Whatever values she held, they openly and loudly rejected—an act, you see, that lessened the impact of what they perceived as *her* rejection of *them.*

She wound up with kids who had spent so much of their precious childhood energy trying to please her, to win some sort of nod of approval, no matter how small, that in the end they went elsewhere for approval and lost much of their ability to function in a healthy, whole, mature manner.

A healthy life is a *balanced* life. Feeling important is one of several priceless nuggets we set on those scales that ultimately weigh our children's chance to live fully, to live morally and uprightly, to live with character.

Into God's heart and hands, then, we place our efforts to develop our children's awareness of their own importance.

Questions for each of us to ask ourselves:

—Do my kids know they are special to me? How do I show them?

—Do I know what my kids are struggling with today? How am I helping them through it?

—Do I show my children my respect for them? In what specific way does each of my children need my recognition?

II

KIDS
WITH
DISCIPLINE

CHAPTER 5

"The Boy Who Ate Cold Burgers"

ONE evening, as a rare suppertime treat, ten-year-old Garrik and his dad, Carl, drove to a hamburger stand not far from their home. Carl sent Garrik in to order while he waited in the car.

Garrik liked being trusted with the money and the order. He was proud when his dad assigned him responsibility.

The order came to ten dollars and a few odd cents. Garrik set a twenty dollar bill on the counter and was handed back some bills and a few loose coins in change. He tucked all the change into his jeans pocket so none of it would be lost. Then he took the bag of hot hamburgers, and he and his dad drove home.

Carl distributed the hamburgers around the kitchen table while Garrik's mother laid out chips and pickles and glasses of milk.

"Oh, Dad, I almost forgot," Garrik said, "here's your change." He put it near his dad's place at the table.

Carl looked again at the hamburgers, then re-counted the money sitting by his plate. Finally he looked at Garrik.

"Is some of this yours?" Carl asked his son.

"Sir?" asked Garrik.

"Is some of this money yours? Did you mix up my money with some you already had?"

Garrik shook his head. "No," he replied, "I didn't have any money except your twenty dollar bill."

"Well, then," said Carl, "we're going to have to go back."

Not understanding what was going on—in fact, con-fused by what was going on—Garrik asked, "What's wrong, Dad?"

"What's wrong," his father answered, "is that we were given too much change. We got a five-dollar bill when we should've been given a single."

Carl rose from the table, leaving the hamburgers there, cooling, and he led Garrik outside to the car.

On the return trip Garrik said, "I don't get it, Dad. So what if we got too much change? I mean, it was their fault, wasn't it? You don't think it was me who did it, do you?"

"You didn't do anything wrong, Garrik," his dad replied. "I'm not blaming you for this mistake, and I don't want you to think I am. No one's to blame, not yet. The point is, we have the hamburgers, and we should be expected to pay for what we have. It's as simple as that."

Garrik didn't say anything further but he was think-ing that such a busy hamburger stand wouldn't miss one or two bucks. What possible difference could it make to them? He bet the hamburger people wouldn't ever notice.

On the other hand, it could make a big difference to his family. They had to scrape for every dollar they had.

Garrik thought about how when he was in first grade, his parents could afford to buy him and his brother only one pair of socks apiece. Every night his mother had washed out their socks and carefully laid them across the radiator to dry. In the morning they were all stiff and weird-looking.

Garrik still remembered how funny they felt when he put them on.

So why was his father refusing to accept the good fortune of being given a few extra bucks by accident? It wasn't like they'd stolen it or anything. No, they had been given it.

What was the big deal, anyway?

Carl looked across the seat of the old Ford. He must have understood something of what Garrik was thinking.

"Listen to me, son," he said. "Somebody—either the people at the restaurant or us—somebody has to pay for those hamburgers sitting on our table at home. Do you understand what I'm saying? Hamburgers don't come free to anybody. Somebody has to pay for them."

Garrik turned to meet his dad's eyes. "It doesn't matter who made the mistake," Carl went on. "The mistake isn't what's important; I don't care about the mistake or about who made it or who didn't make it. I care about what's fair. And what's fair is that whoever eats those hamburgers should pay for them.

"And we're the ones eating them, aren't we?"

He waited for Garrik to acknowledge his question. Slowly Garrik nodded his head.

"Okay then," Carl said, "we're the ones who have to pay for them. That's the way it has to be; that's the way it is. It's simply not right to do anything else."

So Garrik took the extra money back to the restaurant's cashier and told her she'd given him four dollars more than she was supposed to.

Then he went home with his father to eat cold burgers.

Modeling Integrity

The highest form of honesty is integrity, the quality

of being honest with *yourself*. It's captured in this statement: "The measure of your character is in what you would do if you knew you would never be found out."

No one would have discovered Carl had been given too much change, not even Garrik. Garrik hadn't counted the money.

But Carl didn't pocket his hidden "gift." And because he didn't, Carl made a lasting impression on his son.

Integrity—that ability to be honest with ourselves before God—is the epitome of self-discipline. Without integrity, self-discipline is only a pie-in-the-sky dream. It doesn't connect to reality. And if it doesn't connect to reality, it won't—it can't—take shape in a child's life.

In his book *Raising Good Children,* Dr. Thomas Lickona writes:

> Teaching by example . . . has to do with how we lead our lives.

> [But] it's not enough. Kids are surrounded by bad examples. They need our words as well as our actions. They need to see us leading good lives, but they also need to know why we do it. For our example to have maximum impact, they need to know the values and beliefs that lie behind it.

> We need to practice what we preach, but we also need to preach what we practice.

If Carl hadn't both practiced and preached, Garrik probably would have dismissed the moral point. He probably would have thought his dad had some out-of-date notion about what was right and what was wrong.

There *is* a new morality, and it's running rampant in our culture. The new morality is not confined to our kids' peer group. It's thick in adult society too. It came partly out of the sixties, which advanced individual human rights but also fostered disrespect for law and authority and loudly proclaimed the idea that people "should do their own thing." It came partly out of the seventies, which exposed corruption in all walks of life and left people with the feeling that if everybody else is out for himself, why not me?

"The new morality," Thomas Lickona reminds us succinctly, "celebrates self-centeredness and self-indulgence. Grab what you can, because you only go around once."

The old morality, on the other hand, is rooted in the Bible, speaks of respect, of service to others, of sacrifice and resistance to temptation, of moderation in the pursuit of pleasure.

These are not popular notions anymore. Our task—and it's not a simple one—is to make them popular at least within our own families.

An ethical code requires that we not rely on others to impose laws and regulations on us. It requires us to commit to principles of right and wrong by internalizing them.

Of course, following the law because it is the law is by no means wrong, and sometimes it's necessary. But if we as parents only give our kids a list of rules to govern their behavior, we have not given them enough. We need to help our children fully understand and take into their hearts the principle *behind* the law.

Jesus wants us to choose to follow the law because we understand its rightness. He wants us to absorb into every cell and fiber of our beings the moral foundation upon which the law is built. He gave us principles to follow. It's not hard to remember them; there are only two:

> 'Love the Lord your God with all your heart and with all your soul and with all your mind.' This is the first and greatest commandment. And the second is like it: 'Love your neighbor as yourself.' All the Law . . . hang[s] on these two commandments (Matthew 22:37-40).

"Oh, Lord!" goes the anguished cry of the sincere Christian. "Help me love you with all my heart and with all my soul and with all my mind. Help me broaden my limited definition of who my neighbors are so that I can truly—*truly*—love them as I do myself. Help me daily, Lord, with these two seemingly impossible tasks!"

Jesus is after our attitudes, not our behaviors. Once the attitudes are set, he knows the behaviors will follow.

Between us, Fred and I have taught at three different Christian liberal arts colleges. Time and again we have seen students who have been raised super-protectively—I could even say, super-restrictively—arrive at a Christian college, where they continue to live in a well-insulated, almost other-worldly shelter.

When they leave college at around age twenty-two, many of these students are on their own, making their own decisions, shaping the direction of their own lives, for the very first time.

Not all of them know how to handle their newfound freedom. A few become lonely isolates, withdrawing from a world that confuses and terrifies them. Others turn sour and prejudiced toward people outside their "safe" inner circle, that is, toward people unlike themselves.

And a significant number of others begin to embrace the behaviors so rigorously denied them by their parents and by church and school officials. Many young adults from good Christian homes have been controlled so long by external rules and regulations that they know little to nothing about how to exert *inner* control over their lives.

External and internal control work together. They are discipline's co-creators.

Mature individuals recognize the healthy symbiosis of external and internal control. Mature individuals know they live in community. They know that the community's good sometimes requires outward compliance to rules, no matter how they feel personally about the justification for those rules.

We have a stretch of road in our town abounding with unsynchronized stoplights. Every block or two you can count on being stopped by a red light. Naturally this is very frustrating.

Why can't the traffic commission get its act together and give us a stoplight pattern that make sense? I don't know.

But until they do, I have no choice; I must stop at each and every red light. The welfare of the community I live in depends on my compliance with this rule, no matter how ridiculous I may find it. My freedom of choice is gone, as well it should be.

There are times in our lives when strict imposition of external discipline not only can't be avoided, it shouldn't be.

Allowing our children to play in the street until they learn for themselves why we have a rule forbidding play in the street— say, after they've been hit by a car—would be an incredibly irresponsible act of parenting.

If they were still alive to do any of their own thinking, they would surely establish a hard and fast rule—*Stay out of streets! Streets are unsafe for playing!*—and we wouldn't have to enforce it. They would do it on their own.

But at what cost?

The Discipline of Superior Force is exercised when a sergeant tells a private, "You do what I tell you or I'll make you wish you had!" Sometimes a parent must be that sergeant. Sometimes we deliberately put between our children and a danger so big they can't imagine it, a lesser danger that they can imagine, a danger like being yelled at or spanked or sent to their room.

But this stage of discipline is a baby stage, a toddler stage, and if we persist in using it, we will hamper growth and possibly even doom our children to a lifetime of functioning at the baby or toddler level.

If we don't help our children find reasons to adopt a code of ethics when they are young, we will send forth from our doorways young adults who can't think for themselves, who won't take responsibility for their own actions, who will know nothing about making wise choices and who—this is so important!—will have been severely retarded in their opportunities to develop character.

We can (and should) have rules forbidding them to engage in any illegal activity, like driving without a license or under the influence of alcohol. For that matter, we can (and should) forbid all underage drinking whether driving is involved or not. Clearly, our responsibility as parents involves setting limits for our children.

But if we control our children's choices as long as they live with us, I fear that whatever we have attempted to teach will be just about as fleeting as an old summer dandelion. That puff of morality we thought we saw will scatter just as soon as the seasons change and we fade from their daily lives. Our children must choose their behavior from within, not have it imposed from without, or—zap!—it will disappear in a flash.

Ultimately, we want external control to become internal control. We want *our* rules to become *their* rules. We want our children to behave according to the dictates of personal conscience. We want them to choose a behavior because they know that, in God's eyes, it's the right choice to make.

How can we help ensure that our kids internalize the rightness of moral choice? I believe the best way is to be an unforgettable model. Carl modeled his code of ethics to Garrik. He modeled integrity. We can too.

We can also model fair-mindedness. What do our children hear us say about other people? Do they hear us gossip and complain? Do they hear us mock and slander other races, other cultures?

We can model moderation. How do we entertain ourselves on weekends? What do our children see us do in the pursuit of pleasure? What kind of language do they hear us use? What kind of jokes do they hear us tell?

We can model respect for marriage, for family. Are we quick to react with anger? Do we explode at those nearest and dearest to us, yet maintain control of ourselves in front of strangers?

We can model respect for the law. Do we regularly use "fuzz busters" to avoid speed limits? Does our behavior change when we see a police car coming? Do we subtly lift our foot from the accelerator, or, perhaps less subtly, hit the brakes?

If we have integrity, we are honest with ourselves— honest with ourselves before God. Integrity is the highest form of morality there is.

It is also the heart of self-discipline.

Inevitably, our children will make mistakes of judgment. Inevitably, they will fall short of their own standards, not to mention ours.

But I ask you: What better time to make mistakes and learn from them than while they are in our homes, being supported daily by our love and counsel?

Children who have been given freedom over their own behavior, including the freedom to make mistakes; children who come to the point of realizing the value of personal integrity; children who finally measure their character by what they would do if they knew they would never be found out—it is those children who will discipline themselves.

And we (as we should be!) will be out of a job.

Questions for each of us to ask ourselves:
　—What kind of model of integrity am I to my children? Do they see me practicing what I preach, preaching what I practice?
　—How can I improve the consistency of my own behavior? What specific areas do I need to work on?
　—Am I giving my children too little freedom of choice? What can I do to give them more? Am I adjusting their freedom as they grow older?
　—Am I giving too much freedom? What are the limits I will not go beyond? How can I best communicate nonnegotiable outer limits to my children?

CHAPTER 6

"The Boy Who Rescued Birds"

THE morning after a thunderstorm ripped through their front yard, five-year-old Paul brought a nest with five baby birds to his mother. All were upright in their twiggy bed of dried grass, necks outstretched, brown heads bent backward, wide-open mouths cheeping insistently for food.

"Mom," Paul said, cradling his find in his hands and lifting it for his mother to see, "look what I have!"

His mother, Sarah, looked—and couldn't believe what she saw. "What in the world!" It wasn't so much a question as an exclamation. "Where did they come from, Paul? Where did you find them?"

"On the ground," Paul said. "Under the big tree out there." He waved vaguely in the direction of the front yard.

Sarah's eyes followed the movement of her son's hand. "You just found them on the ground? This nest was just sitting there on the ground under the big tree out front?"

Paul nodded, worried that his mother wasn't getting the point. His voice increased in intensity. "Mom," he said, "they're hungry."

Sarah dropped her dishtowel. "Well, of course they are, poor babies! They probably haven't eaten since before the storm started last night." She cleaned off a space at the table. "Here, Paulie," she said, "set them here."

As if they were still in their eggshells, Paul placed the nest of baby birds on the kitchen table and, without taking his eyes from them, asked, "What are we going to feed them, Mom? Worms?"

Sarah thought that over for a moment. "I don't really know," she admitted, not sure she was ready to deal with worms. "Do you think there's anything else baby birds might eat? Of course, the storm last night would've brought some worms up out of the ground. Probably it wouldn't be too hard to find a few."

"I could go look," Paul offered.

"I know you could, sweetheart," agreed his mother, "and it still may come to that, but maybe before we do anything else, I'll see if I can get some expert advice. There's got to be someone who knows more about taking care of baby birds than I do."

Why not go straight to the top, Sarah thought to herself, so she looked up the telephone number for the St. Louis Zoo.

The zoo operator routed her immediately to a bird specialist.

When a man came on the line, he listened to Sarah's story, chuckling. He wasn't the least perturbed at having his morning interrupted. If anything, he was delighted by it.

"Do you know what kind they are?" he asked when she'd finished.

"No," replied Sarah.

She described them. Probably they were robins.

"So what should I do?" Sarah asked. "Try to put them back into the tree?"

"Well, it's not likely their mother'll return to take care of them. Both you and your son have already handled them."

"What are you telling me? That *I'm* in the baby robin business?"

"Something like that," replied the ornithologist cheerfully.

Sarah drew in a deep breath. "Okay, so how does one go about getting into the baby robin business—that is, getting into it *successfully?*"

"I won't lie to you," he answered. "Your ultimate success is pretty much in doubt. They're fragile little creatures who have to be fed round the clock. It's not easy to be a human mother to baby birds."

Sarah groaned. Paul's eyes, wide and hopeful, connected with Sarah's.

"Well, I have to try," she said decisively, "and that's all there is to it. So what do you recommend?"

"Okay, you'll want to make a pulp of ground-up fruit like apples, then add oatmeal or any other non-sugared dried cereal you have around the house. Moisten it with a few drops of cod liver oil and plop it into their mouths with tweezers. Got that?"

"Fruit, oatmeal, cod liver oil—all smushed into a pulp. Yeah," Sarah said, "I've got that."

"Appetizing little mess, isn't it?" The voice on the phone chuckled again. "You'll need to feed them this every hour or so for the next several days."

"Great," Sarah said.

"Who knows? You might actually get them past the critical stage and on their merry ways."

Sarah smiled reassuringly at her son. "Thanks for all your help," she said into the phone.

After a quick run to the drugstore for cod liver oil, Sarah and Paul mixed the strange ingredients into a foul fishy-smelling concoction. Then they settled back to begin playing mama bird to the five little starvelings.

Paul's two-year-old brother, Kenny, contributed much fascinated interest to the project, though little help. Still, Sarah occasionally allowed her youngest son to drop food from the tweezers into the baby birds wide open throats.

Her husband, Frank, got into the act later that evening. In fact, he and Sarah shared wake-up shifts throughout the night.

But most of the daytime responsibility for the feedings was delegated to Paul, who took to the task gladly.

And once a day it was Sarah's job to carefully—and without much joy—lift the robins' little feathered bottoms and clean out their nest.

Four of the baby birds survived until the weekend when a new problem arose. The family was scheduled to attend a church retreat.

"We have no choice," Frank said. "We have to take them with us. They may die if we do, but they'll certainly die if we don't."

So the nest was packed carefully into a box and placed between Paul and Kenny in the backseat of the car for the two-hour drive out to the campground.

Their arrival at the campground was a first for the church. No one remembered ever having a nest of new robins at a weekend retreat before. Along with plenty of excitement came some offers of help and even some prayers for the fragile babies' welfare.

But one by one throughout that Saturday, the baby robins died. No longer could they cope with life's traumas.

Paul was grief-stricken. Sarah held him tightly while he wept.

"It's not easy losing what you love," she said, stroking her son's cheek. "It's all right to cry, Paul. It's all right to miss your baby birds. God knows that, so he gave us eyes that cry. He knows we can't help feeling sad."

"Will I ever see them again?" Paul asked.

"Listen to me, honey," Sarah replied, "when you go to heaven God will make certain you're completely happy. He won't let you be sad in heaven. So if not seeing your baby robins again would make you sad, why, I expect God'll have them in heaven with you. In fact, God may even tell them to fly right up and sit on your shoulder."

"Really?"

"Really."

Frank dug four little holes under a tree at the campground. Each bird was wrapped in tissue, and the family held a private burial.

Frank touched his son's hair. "Do you want to say a prayer for the baby birds?" he asked.

Paul nodded and bowed his head. "Thank you, God, for the baby birds. Thank you for letting them live in our family for a little while. Please feed them real good. And when they get big, please teach them to fly. I want them to sit on my shoulder someday. Amen."

Encouraging Compassion

Sarah and Frank didn't initiate the compassion extended to the birds; Paul did that on his own. They did, however, encourage compassion by welcoming it in Paul when they saw it. Sarah and Frank physically and emotionally joined Paul in caregiving. They thrust the whole family into the middle of it.

And Paul learned through his parents' example that the urgent needs of others take precedence over convenience, that reaching out is more important than any hardships it may bring.

The birds didn't have to survive to make this lesson strong and memorable. All that was required was a genuine effort to better their *chances* of survival.

All that was required was to have an able human family do everything within its power to help a needy animal family.

Every small child I have ever known—and I have known lots and lots of them—finds animals fascinating, if not utterly bewitching. It's only a short trip from caring for animals to caring for human beings.

Paul made that trip. One day several years later, the Jerry Lewis Labor Day Telethon was on television. Paul watched it with growing interest.

He saw children with muscular dystrophy who lived in his town, who went to schools he knew, who drove with their families down the same streets he did.

Here were kids his age who were like him in every way except, of course, that they spent their lives in wheelchairs or with braces roped around their legs.

They spent their lives with almost no motor control over the things Paul took completely for granted, things like putting on shoes or turning his head to smile at a friend.

There was one boy with muscular dystrophy Paul found particularly painful to watch. But watch him he did. It was as if Paul forced himself to understand something of this boy's suffering, to try to feel what it would be like to be this boy if just for a day.

Paul finally decided he couldn't understand even if he were like him just for an hour.

At that point, Paul called the local telephone number moving across the bottom of the screen.

His father, who was working nearby, heard Paul say into the phone, "How do I get to where you're at? I want to bring you some money."

Immediately Frank put away what he was doing and came to stand beside his son.

"I'll take you, Paul," he said. "I know where they are." He waited while Paul collected the money from his small savings bank—all of it, every last dime—and then drove him to the television station.

Paul turned over his money to one of the MD volunteers in the parking lot. When he came back to the car,

Frank said, "That was a neat thing you just did, Paul. I'm proud of you."

What's especially phenomenal about this to me is that Paul *himself* responded to the needs of a stranger.

It wasn't that he gave all his money, or that he gave it to help combat muscular dystrophy. It's that his reaching out to others was guided from *within*. His father didn't suggest it. It was Paul's own inner conviction that set his course of behavior. Frank simply followed Paul's lead.

So one way we can lead our children to compassion is by responding to *their* lead. Children provide such leads all the time. Our job is to notice them, then reward and reinforce them, just as Paul's parents did.

For instance, have you ever noticed how a small child will invariably spring to help when something slips from our hands and drops to the ground? Now there's an opportunity right there. We can let that child know how much his kindness means to us. We can accept with gratitude what she tries to do for us, even if we could manage it better ourselves.

We can also lead our children to compassion by inviting them to come with us when we reach out to others.

One time after I had had surgery, Ida brought our family a pot of homemade soup for dinner. Her young teenaged daughter, Amy, was with her. Included in the gift of food was a pan of brownies baked especially for us by Amy.

Ida dispenses charity as easily as she breathes. But this was the first time I had known Amy to join her mother's ministry. While Amy often rode along in the car with Ida, Ida never forced Amy's involvement. All Ida did was invite Amy to accompany her.

Ida's invitations were persistent, but they weren't insistent.

In her own time, Amy accepted her mother's invitations, and eventually Amy even chose to participate in what her mother was doing.

Another way we can lead children to compassion is to create compassionate moments. Because needy people are all around us, opportunities to exercise compassion are all around us.

At Christmas, through their church, Elaine and Les anonymously adopt a young child whose father is in prison. Then, along with their daughter Meg, these good people shop for presents for the child, selecting toys and pajamas and other items that the child both wants and needs. They wrap the presents and send them on their way—all signed "Merry Christmas from Daddy."

They do all this quietly. The child never meets his or her Santa benefactors. The gifts are shipped anonymously, via a social agency. This is the way Les and Elaine choose to protect the needy family's pride.

Compassion is disciplined into children's lives when small acts of kindness become a family's norm, when tender benevolence is distributed as routinely as smiles.

Like all types of *self*-discipline, compassion doesn't evolve from rigid rules and regulations, from have-to's or an imposition of guilt. Compassion isn't cajoled or threatened into being. It doesn't appear because someone else forces it upon us.

It comes, in its truest form, from *within.*

And like every other type of self-discipline, we need it. All of us—you, I, our kids—all of us need to practice the inner discipline that, at times, allows us to give mercy and, at other times, to receive it.

Compassion is one of the most exquisite and essential elements of life. None of us would choose to live in a world devoid of it; probably none of us could.

For it is in compassion, both in its giving and in its receiving, that every human being is brought nearer to the heart of God.

Questions for each of us to ask ourselves:

—Do I understand the importance of living a compassion-ate life? Truly?

—Do I model compassion? Have my children ever "caught" me in a compassionate act?

—Do my children sometimes give me openings that I fail to respond to? What can I do to become more aware of the openings they give?

CHAPTER 7

"The Aunt Whose Wisdom Bought Flowers"

Lukas's fourth birthday would be in three more weeks, but today he wasn't thinking of birthdays or presents or cake and ice cream. Today he was thinking of his new baby sister.

Five days ago Lukas's mommy, lumbering alongside his daddy, had kissed him good-bye and told him the next time she saw him she'd have a new baby for him. Lukas wondered how long that would take.

That night his Aunt Jolie read him stories and played games with him. She fixed him a snack and then—finally—she put him to bed.

Well, today his baby sister Shanda was five days old. Today was the day she and Lukas's mommy finally would come home from the hospital. Today was the day Lukas would be able to see them. Today was the day he could hug Mommy and hold Shanda.

That morning when he woke up, Aunt Jolie took Lukas to the hospital. Lukas's daddy was there, and he told Lukas about his new baby sister.

Aunt Jolie told him that once upon a time she'd been waiting in a hospital lobby pretty much like this one. She'd been waiting to see *her* baby sister, his mother.

This interested Lukas enormously. "My mommy was your baby sister?"

"Yes, Luke, she was," Aunt Jolie said. "Your mommy was my baby sister."

"What did she look like?"

"Well, she was very, very tiny—so tiny she almost couldn't wrap all her fingers around just one of mine. She slept a lot, and she cried a lot, and I loved her very, very much."

"Will Shanda look like my mommy did?"

"I imagine so, Luke. I imagine Shanda will look very much like your mommy did. She'll be tiny, and you'll have to touch her very carefully, and she'll sleep a lot and cry a lot. That's the way babies are. That's the way you were when you were a baby."

"Did you know me when I was a baby?"

"I sure did, Luke. You were such a cute baby. I used to hold you and rock you and sing songs to you."

"You did?"

"Yes, I did—and now that's what we'll both do with Shanda. Won't that be fun?"

They sat side by side on stiff plastic seats in the lobby of the hospital. Somewhere in the hidden upper regions above them, Lukas's father was off collecting Mommy and Shanda.

Aunt Jolie wondered if she was up to the nearly impossible task of keeping Lukas's excitement under control. He squirmed and wiggled and jumped beside her on the muddy tan of the slick seats. Beneath his restless weight the seats squeaked and popped.

"Will Mommy come out of those elebaytors?" he asked. "See them, Aunt Jolie? They're right over there."

"Yes, I see them, Luke, and yes, she will. She'll come out of those elevators, but she'll be in a wheelchair."

"What's a wheelchair?"

"Well, it's a chair with wheels on it. A nurse will push her so she won't have to walk."

"Why? Did she hurt her legs?"

"No, Luke, she didn't hurt her legs, but she's tired. Having a baby is hard work."

"Will the baby be with her?"

"Yes, Luke. The baby will be with her."

And that brought up The Question of the Hour again. "What will the baby look like?"

"She'll be wrapped in a blanket," Aunt Jolie said for the forty-first time, "so you won't be able to see much of her at first. And she'll look so tiny you might think she's nothing but a toy."

"But she's not, is she, Aunt Jolie?" He'd heard this before too. "She's not a toy. She's real, isn't she?"

"Yes, Luke, she's very real."

"Will she know who I am?"

"Of course she will. You're her big brother, aren't you? How could she not know who you are?"

Lukas liked this answer. With renewed animation, he wiggled up and down on the seat.

"What will Mommy look like?" he asked then.

"Just the same as she always has, Luke," replied Aunt Jolie, "only she won't be fat anymore. The baby was making her fat, but now of course the baby's not in her. Now the baby's out. Remember I told you how the doctors helped Mommy get the baby out?"

"Yeah," said Lukas. "I know all that stuff, Aunt Jolie. You don't have to tell me again."

"Here," Aunt Jolie said, opening her bag and rummaging inside for her change purse. "Let's take this money and go get you some candy. What would you say to some candy, Luke?"

He nodded happily. "Yeah, candy!"

Aunt Jolie pressed some coins into Lukas's small palm and led him to the hospital gift shop. "Pick what you want, Luke, and then give the lady your money."

Lukas pressed up against the glass case to better see all the selections.

There were red licorice twizzlers and chocolate-covered peanuts. There were Butterfinger bars and Baby Ruths and Snickers. There was all kinds of bubble gum—grape, strawberry, banana, even root beer. There were Tootsie Pops and Milk Duds and Reeses Pieces and Peter Paul Mounds and Hershey Kisses.

The saleslady smiled at her little customer. "What would you like to have, dear?" she asked kindly.

It was then he saw what was next to her. Behind two large refrigerated doors was an array of fresh-cut flowers. There seemed to be as many flower selections as there were candy selections.

"Look, Aunt Jolie!" said Lukas excitedly, pointing to the flowers.

Aunt Jolie looked. "Yes," she said. "They're beautiful, aren't they?"

"Mommy likes flowers," he told her.

"I know she does," Aunt Jolie said. "There's probably nothing more beautiful than flowers."

"Yeah," Lukas agreed solemnly, "there's prob-ly nothing more bood-full than flowers."

He seemed to weigh the coins in his hand for a moment, and then he pressed them—all of them—onto the counter above the candy shelves.

"I'd like some flowers for my mommy, please," he announced to the saleslady.

The saleslady's eyebrows went up, and her inquisitive glance settled on Aunt Jolie.

Aunt Jolie, without hesitation, asked, "Which color would you like, Luke?"

"All colors!"

"Please wrap one of each color," instructed Aunt Jolie. "Luke wants to give his mother a very special gift of love."

"Well, I'd say," the saleslady agreed. She took all of Lukas's coins and put them into the cash register drawer.

Aunt Jolie looked at the few cents difference between Lukas's coins and the price of the flowers. Quietly she placed that amount on the counter.

"This is the most amazing sale I've ever made," said the saleslady while she extracted the flowers from the display and wrapped them. Then she ceremoniously placed them into Lukas's waiting hands.

"Say, 'Thank you,' Luke," Aunt Jolie prompted.

"Thank you!" Lukas sang out, but his eyes were on the bouquet of carnations. There were four flowers wrapped in green tissue. One was red, one yellow, one pink, and the last was white.

When his mother eventually emerged from the elevator door, Lukas ran to her, his excitement no longer containable. It spilled all over his mother.

"For you, Mommy!" he shouted.

And he thrust the flowers bought with his candy money into her hands.

Giving Selflessly

Aunt Jolie could have destroyed Lukas's precious, priceless gift. All she had to do was say, "Here, Luke, let me buy the flowers. I gave you that money for candy. But if you use it for flowers you won't get any candy, so let me buy the flowers for you to give to Mommy, okay?"

Fortunately for Lukas, Aunt Jolie was wise enough not to do to her nephew what many of us would have done had we been in her shoes. She did not operate blindly from a misguided, misplaced notion of what "kindness" means.

Instead, she allowed Lukas to experience the thrill of giving. She put no temptations in his path that might have caused him to stumble from his expression of pure, selfless love.

Selfless acts of love are rare for the best of us. But they're exceedingly rare for small children who are more into yelling, "Mine!" than they are into foregoing candy so someone else can have flowers.

This is altruism at its simplest and most beautiful. And its spirit says something to all of us. Selflessness liberates. It frees us from our constant self-absorption and allows us to get outside ourselves.

Fred is a model of selflessness in our home. He is always giving, mostly to me. Our children can't help but see that. In fact, they witness it constantly.

Fred grabs the grocery list off the refrigerator and runs to the store; he pulls out the vacuum cleaner and sweeps the floor; he throws a hunk of meat in the crock-pot in the morning; he brings me my coffee when I first awaken; he sorts the laundry, puts it in the washing machine, folds it when it's dry.

He's always saying, "Let me get that," or, "Let me do that." I'm a lucky, lucky wife. Believe me, I'm the first to admit it. While I certainly appreciate Fred's tangible gifts of love, I neither ask for them nor expect them.

He chooses to give them to me.

But what Fred is giving our sons is even stronger, even more important. He's giving them this message: I love your mother.

What a wonderful message for two future husbands! Fred's model of selfless love has spanned many years. It's not just what he does, it's that he repeatedly does it. His pattern is continual, on record. It has weathered time.

We can perform lots of little selfless acts for our children. We can bring them the peanuts off our flights. We can surprise them by doing one of their weekly chores; we can pitch in and help them with a huge job like cleaning out their closet, instead of requiring them to tackle it alone.

We can give to others outside our home. Two families in our church rotate bringing a handicapped man to worship services and Sunday school each and every week. They do this without fail. They have for years. They are models for their children—and for the rest of us—of pure, selfless giving.

If we are consistent in our model, over time our children will absorb it. Gordon did.

Gordon was a high school sophomore whose math teacher was truly horrible. Since Gordon was classified as gifted, his parents had some legal rights. They could demand, and win, changes in Gordon's educational placement.

Gordon was scheduled to be removed from his math class and placed into another. But because he was the only "gifted" kid in the class, he was also the only one the principal planned to remove.

Gordon's good friend Ryan was in the same class. What was helping both Gordon and Ryan survive the destructive tendencies of their teacher was their togetherness. If Gordon left the class, Ryan would be alone.

Gordon refused to leave. He stayed in the math class and suffered through the year, side by side with Ryan.

When we give to others, when we care for them—really care for them—we grow. Husbands and wives grow when they care for their mates, parents grow when they care for their children, teachers grow when they care for their students, writers grow when they care for their ideas. Lukas grew when he cared for his mother; Gordon grew when he cared for his friend.

Behaving selflessly, we are more of everything—more aware, more responsive, more mentally healthy.

Mentally healthy people operate at their highest potential and focus their energy in ways that best develop them as human beings. They experience each moment fully, vividly, and with full concentration. They think of life as a process of choices—their choices. They listen to their inner voice and trust it; they take responsibility for themselves; they dare to be different, nonconforming, real. They open up to themselves, identify their defenses, and find the courage to give them up.

Attaining good mental health is a process of life growth. It's a process of becoming more internally whole. Milton Mayeroff, in his little book *On Caring,* says it this way: "Besides the other's need for me if it is to grow, I need the other to care for if I am to be myself." Helping others helps us to become more of who God intended us to be.

How does this square with our litigious society, with a contentious culture that is forever demanding its rights, that is forever shouting, "Me, me, me!"?

It doesn't. Our society, if we let it, will cripple our children. It will actually stunt their growth.

Let's talk about these things in our homes. Let's consciously, specifically point out to our children that we don't lose ourselves when we give to others; we *gain* ourselves. Let's tell them that rather than becoming less, we become more.

The Bible is filled with confirmation of this. In Luke 6:38 Jesus promised, "Give, and it will be given to you. A good measure, pressed down, shaken together and running over, will be poured into your lap."

Paul, in Acts 20:35, wrote, "In everything I did, I showed you that . . . we must help the weak, remembering the words the Lord Jesus himself said: 'It is more blessed to give than to receive.' "

Caring for others, giving selflessly to them, is not an emptying, it's a filling.

A wise aunt knew this. She knew that eating candy wouldn't fill Lukas. Buying flowers for his mother with his candy money would.

Perhaps, on the surface, we could think of Aunt Jolie as cold or unkind. After all, she didn't give Lukas extra money so that he would have enough for both candy and flowers.

Lukas's gift to his mother looked like a sacrifice, even a supreme sacrifice. Lukas didn't think so.

He didn't regret what he left behind in the gift shop, not even once. The flowers in his hand provided the momentum needed to drive him joyfully forward. Only from our perspective, and from his mother's, is it sacrificial. It brings tears to our eyes and lumps to our throats.

The examples of Lukas and Gordon and others are undeniably touching and memorable, even noble, and because they are, we can learn from them. A lovely act can teach us something about the Author of Lovely Acts.

"God's method is always incarnational," Howard G. Hendricks writes in *Teaching to Change Lives*. "He loves to take his truth and wrap it in a person."

Sometimes he wraps that truth in a very small person, in someone very young.

And sometimes—oh, happy day!—an Aunt Jolie is there to recognize it and pass on its message to the rest of us.

Questions for each of us to ask ourselves:
    —Do I only preach the merits of selflessness, or do I model them too?
    —When was the last time I modeled selflessness? How did I do it?
    —Am I doing enough to cultivate selflessness in my children? In what specific ways can I improve?

CHAPTER 8

"The Family That Added a Stranger"

ROGER and Mitchell were teenaged brothers whose grandfather boarded with an old woman in a large house in the seediest, most rundown part of town. At one time its row of white clapboard houses sat in a fairly normal middle-class neighborhood, but those days were long gone. Now the street was dark, strewn with debris, lined with boarded-over, roach- and rat-infested houses.

The boys' parents tried repeatedly to get Grandpa Joe to move in with them. He always refused. He liked the independence of living away from family.

Grandpa Joe's landlady, Lettie Reuben, was considerably older than her boarder, and he himself was plenty old to begin with. Or at least that's how Roger and Mitchell saw it.

But they also knew Mrs. Reuben was kindly and took very good care of Grandpa Joe.

She always had freshly laundered, starched and pressed shirts for him to wear. Each day she provided three plain but filling home-cooked meals. She was Grandpa Joe's foil in his beloved cribbage games. And she was his companion at night, a comfortable presence who uncomplainingly sat with him and watched an old flickering black-and-white TV.

Of course, Grandpa Joe took good care of Mrs. Reuben too. He wrapped her water pipes in cold weather and tinkered with her balky furnace, somehow cajoling it into belching out enough heat to keep them both warm. He painted the rotting eaves under her roof. He mowed what was left of her grass with an old push mower, trimmed her hedges, raked her leaves.

Grandpa Joe was Mrs. Reuben's all-purpose, live-in handyman. She was his cook and laundress. They had an arrangement that offered contentment and security to them both.

Then one fall Grandpa Joe died, just like that, and the old woman was left alone in her aging house.

Roger and Mitchell attended Grandpa Joe's funeral with their parents, shook hands with Mrs. Reuben, and pretty much thought that was the end of it.

They were wrong.

"Mrs. Reuben is all alone now," said the boys' father at supper one Friday evening.

Their mother wiped her mouth with her napkin. "I worry about her," she said.

"Me too," their father replied. "I think we need to do something."

"The weather's starting to get nippy," said their mother. "Maybe you and the boys could go across town and make sure she's warm enough. Dad always cranked up her furnace, you know."

"I was remembering that too," their father said. "We'll go right after supper tonight."

Mitchell, the more vocal of the two brothers, and the one who had already made a date with his girlfriend for later that evening, offered his opinion. "Isn't that kind of rude or something? I mean, she doesn't know us, and we don't know her. We gotta respect her feelings, don't we?

We gotta be aware how a bunch of strange people coming into her house is likely to make her feel, don't we?''

Roger shoved a forkful of mashed potatoes into his mouth. *Great, Mitch,* he silently cheered. *Way to go, bud.*

Their father's eyes rested thoughtfully on Mitchell. ''Well,'' he said, ''maybe it is kind of late tonight. It'd take us an hour or so to get there, and I expect she goes to bed fairly early. Most older people do.''

Both boys started letting out their breath. Prematurely, as it happened.

''So we'll go first thing in the morning,'' their dad went on. ''That'll give us more time to do whatever jobs need doing.''

And thus began a pattern of care that would last for the next several years and would ''rob'' Roger and Mitchell of many, many Saturdays.

After Roger and Mitchell started college, their parents continued to expect them to donate several days of their school holidays to household service at Mrs. Reuben's. One entire Thanksgiving vacation, for instance, was spent painting her house.

The work plans were matter-of-factly announced when Roger and Mitchell arrived home, and that was that. No arguments accepted. If it was right, you did it. If it was right, what was there to debate?

The two brothers didn't particularly like it, but they did begin to recognize that their parents were more involved than they were—their dad called Mrs. Reuben every morning to make certain she was all right, and their mother called her every evening.

It started seeming petty and mean to be reluctant to lend a helping hand to an old woman who obviously needed help.

They never forgot the lesson in commitment their parents consistently, tirelessly, gladly modeled for them.

In fact, they took it into their own marriages. Roger and his wife adopted a fatherless, all but homeless family and took the children on outings to the zoo, on picnics, to ball games and movies.

Mitchell and his wife adopted a lonely old man in a nursing home and visited him regularly, remembering him with small gifts on his birthday and holidays.

Cultivating Commitment

It's hard to write an ending for this story. As far as I can see, there isn't any. That's one of the beauties of this kind of teaching.

We applaud others who make long-term commitments but we often find it difficult to make them ourselves. Sometimes we have to be forced into it, to be given no choice.

Neil Postman calls the age we live in "The Age of Show Business." Entertainment is the quest of modern times. More than that, it's *passive* entertainment we're after—that is, the kind we sit back and watch rather than the kind we do.

Television's frightening takeover of our lives is discussed at length in Postman's book, *Amusing Ourselves to Death.*

In this day and age we seldom actively engage in our *own* lives, not to mention anybody else's. That makes teaching our children about commitment all the more difficult, wouldn't you say?

As humans, we function best in community. None of us can successfully live our lives alone. A gathering of couch-potatoes, each inhabiting its own little box on the planet, is considerably less than a community.

It's not really a community at all. Nothing unifies it into a community. There's no involvement with other people's real lives. It's all play-acting. It's just distorted video images.

Commitment comes from being involved—really and truly involved—in the lives of others. And it comes from realizing that those we're committed to are just as involved in our lives as we are in theirs.

The reason we teach our children to commit to others isn't so that we, as parents, can be complimented on how nice and polite or well-mannered our children are, what pleasant and sweet social graces they have. Our commitment to community is to bring about social responsibility, not social acceptability.

My son Kyle made a commitment one summer to umpire Little League baseball games. He got so much verbal abuse from overly-competitive parents, I was the one who wanted him to break his commitment.

Sometimes I would sit in the stands and watch him, hoping that my presence might provide some sort of protection for him. It was a foolish mother's delusion; I knew it even then.

But, I reasoned, maybe, at the very least, Kyle would feel less isolated, less like a lonely lamb among wolves if he could look out from under his home plate mask and see a familiar, friendly smile beaming at him from the stands.

Kyle's knowledge of baseball is vast. He was a good, fair, calm umpire that summer, and he knew it. He was there for the boys, he told me, those young seven-year-old players, not for their parents.

Since his pay was negligible (though no amount of pay would have made up for the abuse he took!), his commitment was solely to the boys on each team. Whenever Kyle made a call, he'd unfailingly tell the players involved the rule behind the call and the reasoning behind the rule.

He was a patient, likable teacher who went unrecognized and unappreciated by most of those boys' parents.

Who would be there if he wasn't? Kyle would ask. Who was to say what his replacement might be like? What if someone new didn't bring the same spirit of concern to umpiring that he did? What then?

I couldn't answer that. I didn't know. But I saw Kyle's point and blessed him for keeping a commitment under trying circumstances.

Teenagers do remarkable things all the time. We need to note them. One teenager I know gave up a ski trip to Colorado's Rocky Mountains because she'd already made a commitment to her forensics team during her spring break.

Another, believe it or not, gave up a trip to Europe when his football team was selected for an end-of-season championship tournament. He wasn't a first-stringer, played rarely or for only a few minutes at a time, but he still felt—rightly, I think—that his place was with his team.

His sacrifice, his *commitment*, energized his teammates, sparked them onward, and they won the first-place trophy.

When our kids choose not to break the trust of those with whom they have forged commitments—parents, siblings, friends, teachers, employers, whomever—they are well on the road to being socially responsible.

And when they're well on that road, self-discipline's right there beside them. Count on it.

But, my, commitment's hard! It takes hanging in there through lots of rough stuff, and we don't live in times that preach much toleration for rough stuff. This is an increasingly "that's-enough-of-that-see-ya-later" society. Staying committed often requires ignoring strong feelings reeling inside us.

So how do we create commitment in our kids? There's no hard and fast answer. Kids get so many conflicting messages from the world beyond our doors that all I can say is we must try our level best not to add to the confusion. At the very least, let's have the messages sent from our homes consistent and committed and tuned in to the needs of people we're involved with, even if the world's messages aren't.

If our kids want to take piano lessons or learn to play the trumpet, let's make sure they practice regularly and get to their lessons on time. Help them understand that their teachers are depending on them. Then praise them when they follow through.

If our kids want to sing in the church choir or join Scouts, let's make sure they go to rehearsals and participate in meetings. Help them understand that their leaders are depending on them. Then praise them when they follow through.

If our kids want to go to a party with their friends, let's make sure they report where it will be, who will be there, and what time they will be home. Help them understand that we are depending on them to follow through. And, of course, we must praise them when they do.

Our kids can't strain out from life the parts they don't like in order to have the parts they do like, and we shouldn't in any way imply that they can. No one can have the thrill of wearing an Eagle Scout badge without first sitting through lots and lots of boring blue-and-gold banquets.

When our son Marc decided he wanted to be a West Point cadet, his father penned these wise, helpful lines:

MOST MEN HAVE DREAMS.
SOME MEN SET GOALS FOR THEMSELVES.
ONLY A FEW PAY THE PRICE TO ACHIEVE THEM.
GO FOR IT!

Fred then went to a professional print shop, had this message emblazoned onto dozens of posters, and hung them all around our house for Marc to see daily.

Nothing "comes true" for any of us unless we first make a personal commitment to it.

We can pledge to commitments individually, and we can pledge to commitments as a family.

Some families, like ours, have hosted a foreign exchange student. This is, to say the least, a challenging commitment. It's difficult; it disrupts routines; it poses communication hazards; it changes cultural norms.

It adds complexity to already complex lives.

But I promise you, it's well worth all risk involved—even if the experience turns out less than ideally.

Through the problems of adjustment, families learn flexibility. Through problems, we learn to focus on solutions. Through problems, if we truly commit to seeing them through, we learn to turn what's unpleasant into strength and cohesion, into family unity.

I call this "freedom in a fenced yard." Within the fence my children can have all the freedom to roam that they want. I won't tell them which plot of ground they can play on and which they can't. Those are their choices.

But responsibility to others is one of the things that denies them *unlimited* freedom.

We erect fenceposts when we make commitments to other people, when we live, as we should, in community. The fencing strung between the posts marks the outer limits of personal behavior. Commitment pledges us to respect those limits.

Our word, our commitment to others, may bind us to limits, but we don't have to see these limits as bad or negative. And I surely don't want my children seeing it that way.

Yes, commitment curtails our freedom to act.

But it also gives us freedom *to be.*

Questions for each of us to ask ourselves:
—What commitments do my children see me make? What commitments do my children see me keep? Do I consistently honor my commitments?

—How have I helped my kids keep their word? In what specific ways do I encourage them? Could I do more? What?

—Do I involve my children with me in pledging to *family* commitments? How?

III

KIDS
WITH
LEADERSHIP

CHAPTER 9

"The Boy Who Ejected His Teammate"

A young adolescent in the summer between his seventh and eighth grade years, a true kid of the fifties, Andy was an avid baseball fan. In particular, he loved his hometown Kansas City A's. Nearly every day he would ride the bus across town to Municipal Stadium where he would settle into a seat—cap on head, glove in hand—in the outfield bleacher section.

But Andy wasn't only a big league fan; he was also the star catcher on his neighborhood Little League team. Furthermore, he was a valued member of his Baptist church's Bible quiz team.

A young all-American boy, Andy spent his summer afternoons in ballparks and his summer evenings in the church parlor. What more could you ask of a twelve-going-on-thirteen-year-old kid?

His heroes—those stars of the large green downtown diamond where Andy spent so much of his time—would sometimes gather together and pray in the dugout or in the locker room. They did this more commonly before a big game, often during the World Series.

But it didn't matter to Andy when they did it; what mattered to him was *that* they did it. The sight of those athletic all-grown-up men unashamedly praying together moved him.

It made such an impression on a young impressionable mind that Andy resolved to organize something similar with his own team.

One night he called together all but one of his teammates and told them he thought they should conduct a team prayer. So, precisely as Andy suggested, they all settled down to do it.

Andy liked the feeling of having his friends grouped around in a solemn circle, heads bowed and hands clasped, while he invoked God's help on their behalf. It was a strong moment. There was a manly tone, invigorating to adolescent boys, but it was appropriately tempered by the love of Christ, and Andy was glad to have been the one who thought to make it happen.

He was so glad about his role in it that that night when his mother, Katherine, came into his room to give her usual good night kiss, he told her about it.

Opening up to her in this way was not especially characteristic of Andy and that he did so now surprised Katherine.

"You called the team together for prayer?" she asked.

Andy nodded. "Yes," he said.

"That's terrific, Andy!" she said. "It's really neat that you would have thought to organize a team prayer. Everyone was there?"

Andy nodded again. "Well," he conceded after a moment, "everyone except Tim."

"Oh? Not Tim?" Katherine looked closely at her son. "Why wasn't Tim there?"

"I didn't invite him."

Andy had no qualms about revealing this to his mother. He was sure she would understand when he told her why.

She gave him an opening almost immediately. "Why didn't you invite Tim?"

"This was a Christian prayer, Mom," Andy said matter-of-factly. "Don't you remember? Tim's Catholic. I couldn't invite a Catholic to pray with us. Our prayer was just for all us *Christian* guys."

Katherine sat on the edge of the bed beside her son. "Andy," she said, "I'm very proud of how you decided to get the team together to have a prayer. That shows lots of leadership and caring. You've surprised me in a very happy way, and I thank you for that."

She reached over and kissed Andy's forehead as he rested on his pillow. Then she went on. "There is one thing that bothers me, though."

Andy's brow furrowed. "What's that?" he asked, genuinely puzzled.

"Well," replied Katherine, "it bothers me that you didn't include Tim. In fact, it bothers me quite a lot."

"Huh?" Andy stared at his mother blankly. "*That* bothers you? But why, Mom? Don't you know that Tim's Catholic?"

"Yes, I know Tim's Catholic," she said. "But it bothers me that you think Catholics can't be Christians. How do you know Tim's not a Christian? Have you asked him?"

Andy's eyes popped wide open. "He can't be, Mom!" he protested. "He eats fish every Friday night. His church makes him!"

Katherine suppressed a smile. "I know," she said. "But what any of us does or doesn't do isn't what makes us Christian, Andy; it's what we believe that does that. Have you asked Tim what he believes about Jesus?"

Andy shook his head slowly. "So I should've talked to Tim, and if he said he believed in Jesus, I should've invited him to be part of the team prayer?"

"Well, yes and no," Katherine answered. "I think it's always good to talk about Jesus.

"But," she went on, "whether your friends are Christians or not, I don't think you should exclude them from the team prayer. In fact, I don't think you should exclude *anyone* from praying with you, ever."

Katherine bent over and kissed Andy one more time. "Good night, Andy," she said. "I love you. I'm really proud of what you did today. You have courage and commitment, and those are a couple of terrific things to have."

Producing Initiative

Andy needed two things from his mother. He needed her to genuinely praise him for his initiative and gently admonish him for his attitude toward Tim. Lucky for Andy, those were the very two things Katherine did.

Children look sturdy on the outside but this outward robustness can, and often does, camouflage an inner fragility. Emotionally, our children are vulnerable. We have tremendous power to enhance or destroy their emotional well-being.

Katherine used her power wisely. She dealt with Andy in a kind and caring way. Through her response she commended Andy's initiative in getting the team together for prayer.

Katherine didn't ignore a teachable moment. She created it. And in so doing, she enabled her son sometime in the future to undertake yet more important acts of initiative.

Psychologist Erik Erikson delineated eight major dilemmas that all of us, universally, experience over the course of our lifetimes.

Each of these eight psychological crises has a positive or desirable pole, which represents social maturity, and each has a negative or undesirable pole, representing social immaturity. Social immaturity must be resolved, dealt with, eliminated, if we're to grow wise, capable minds.

Erikson's third crisis, the one he labels *Initiative versus Guilt,* is the stage pertinent to our discussion here.

At the *Initiative versus Guilt* stage, children's growing sense of independence drives them into new and complex social situations. In other words, initiative is what challenges our children to master new learning tasks.

They develop it naturally. It's almost intuitive. Children delight in initiating activities that test their capacities, that help them define their present and future roles. What's more, they frequently try to get others to join them in these activities. They act on an impulse and gladly influence others to act right along with them.

Fletcher and his friend Skip want to put on a play. They ask Fletcher's parents for props—a flashlight, a blanket, a roll of tape.

Fletcher's parents can say, "Maybe later. I don't have time to look for those things right now."

Or Fletcher's parents can find the props, hand them over with a smile, and say, "Tell me when the play's ready. I'd like to sit in the audience, if you don't mind."

From the time they are small, children seek to find ways to help us, to be independent and assertive, to participate completely and autonomously as fully functioning family members. The conflict at Erikson's third stage is between searching for this sense of initiative and knowing that sometimes we all attempt things beyond what we can or should handle. Initiative is developed by an opportunity to make mistakes.

A very young child drops and breaks dishes while eagerly helping set the table; a girl home from school decides to surprise the family by cooking dinner and, instead, burns up her mother's best pan; a boy voluntarily fills the lawn mower with gasoline and, in the process, spills some on the grass, killing it.

Each youngster miscalculated his or her capabilities. Each one was a victim of misplaced enthusiasm. Each one initiated a good action that went awry.

And each one, count on it, feels guilty, ashamed, inept. We can heighten their feelings of inadequacy by saying, "Gracious, but you're clumsy! How many times have I told you not to carry so many things at once?"

We can heighten their shame by saying, "Now look what you've gone and done! I told you you couldn't do that. Next time maybe you'll listen to me."

Next time maybe they will.

Capitalizing on our children's feelings of guilt is a frightful practice. It squelches initiative. Children robbed of their initiative evolve into fearful or apathetic creatures—who then evolve into fearful or apathetic adults.

Such people wait nervously for others to take command. Inhibited in their ability to think for themselves, they wait for someone else to tell them how to act and feel, what to do and believe.

This tension blocks initiative. The first step in releasing initiative is to reduce tension, to create a more accepting climate in our homes and classrooms. Adults can choose to encourage or discourage initiative in children, to free their innate leadership or to imprison it. Angelina's parents chose to free leadership and allow it to grow.

Early one Sunday morning, Denise called Angelina and asked if she wanted to go to breakfast before Sunday school. Angelina's parents were used to having breakfast together as a family; nevertheless they thought this was a terrific thing for the two girls to do. Denise didn't normally go to church.

So they encouraged Denise's initiative (and Angelina's too) by providing money for the outing.

The two girls' breakfast get-togethers went on for a few weeks, almost becoming something of a Sunday morning ritual. But eventually Angelina took the initiative and invited Denise over to her house for a pre-church breakfast. Denise accepted.

Before long, several high school girls were coming over to Angelina's house for breakfast and then, together, going on to church.

A new fellowship time was created from the germ of one girl's lead. One person's initiative flowed into another's.

That's the beauty of the creative spirit. And it could be happening all the time.

Three junior high boys were distressed that their classmates didn't better support the school basketball team. So they decided to paint their faces with the school colors and wear them the day before each game.

The principal was so amused by and appreciative of this novel display of school spirit that he offered them materials and a free lunch if they would use their lunch period to make banners and posters to hang around the building. They did.

Attendance at the games slightly improved, but school spirit improved a lot.

Reggie was a quiet eighth grade kid whose grades never earned much notice. Neither did his golf game, for the simple reason that he didn't know how to play golf.

It was no surprise, then, that Doug, Reggie's history teacher and the school's golf coach, paid scant attention to the boy. But one day Reggie started asking Doug lots of little golfing questions.

Reggie was curious; that was obvious. It was Reggie who initiated these brief, tentative conversations.

But it was Doug who responded to them.

"One of these days," Doug said, "I'll take you out after school to one of the municipal courses, and we'll play a few holes together. What do you say?"

Reggie said yes. And so they did.

Reggie's grades improved in Doug's history class—nothing great, but enough to notice. And Reggie started being less quiet, more openly curious, more confident of himself.

All because Doug responded to Reggie's initiative. We produce initiative when we reward it by returning it, by accepting what's been presented to us and expanding on it.

"Hey, I like what you did," we say. "That idea's so good, in fact, here's some more of the same back at you."

Our children come into the world cloaked in leadership's mantle. They are born curious. The urge to initiate is intuitive. They have a will to know and understand, to exert leadership over their lives.

Just watch very young children explore their universe. Watch them crawl or toddle through a room. They reach, they touch, they taste; they examine intently. They don't wait to be told where to head; they initiate their own headings. They decide what they want to know more about and determinedly go straight for it.

Our main job as parents is to provide an environment full of safe exploration, then sit back and keep an eye on things. We are there to guide and protect, to describe, perhaps demonstrate, and if it does no harm, to take whatever interests our children off its shelf and place it directly into their hands.

We don't have to plant leadership in our kids; God already has. Our task is to cultivate what's been planted. Our task is to encourage that seedling, to respond to the leads our children will inevitably tamp into the fertile soil of our homes.

Questions for each of us to ask ourselves:
—Do I like it when my children show initiative? Do I allow much of it? How might I be stifling it?
—Do I view myself as self-motivated and initiating? On what do I base this opinion?
—Do I reward initiative in my children? How? Can I encourage its further development? In what specific way?

CHAPTER 10

"The Girl Who Created a Dog Show"

ELLEN was born a Yankee. That is, she lived in the northern United States until she was seven years old. Then her family moved to Greenville, South Carolina.

The year was 1953.

Now, the North was by no means free of racism but at the time that Ellen's family moved to South Carolina, it wasn't as openly racist as the Deep South. In the Deep South, even a white child noticed things.

There were, for instance, signs on every city bus. COLORED TO THE REAR, they said.

There were signs over drinking fountains. If it was a filthy white porcelain fountain eking out tepid water, inevitably it was labeled COLORED. If it was the new refrigerated kind just then becoming popular, it announced WHITE ONLY.

Ellen noticed waiting rooms, too. If they were dark, unlit, windowless, they were sure to have above their doorways one lonely word: COLORED. But if they were modern and clean and filled with bright fluorescent lighting, those ubiquitous signs invariably read: WHITE ONLY.

Some restaurants admitted blacks through the back door. Most didn't admit them at all.

Certainly there were no black children in Ellen's school, though she once saw a black chain gang, wearing striped pajamas and iron balls and chains, laying the road that ran in front of her school.

Her mother broke her wrist one summer and while she healed, a black woman named Hattie came to help out with the daily household tasks. Never before had anyone even close to resembling a "maid" been in their home. Hattie was the first.

Hattie helped out with the cooking as well as with the laundry and ironing. While Ellen was shy around her, she was also curious.

Did Hattie's skin feel the same as white people's? Why were her hands two shades, dark on top and light underneath? Did her family once belong to some rich plantation people? Did her family wear off the color of their palms by picking cotton?

Did she mind sitting at the back of the bus when she rode it to their house in the white neighborhood?

When Hattie would fix lunch, she would set the family's places in the dining room. Then she would retire to the kitchen to eat her own lunch by herself.

Phyllis, Ellen's mother, asked Hattie to come join the rest of the family in the dining room. But she never would. So Phyllis would order her children to collect their plates and move to the kitchen table with Hattie.

Hattie seldom talked. She would sit there, surrounded by Phyllis and the children, and eat her lunch in silence.

One day, after thinking long and hard on the strange black/white racial divisions she saw everywhere around her, Ellen decided to write a book.

Books were Ellen's great love. Phyllis would curl all her children up next to her and read aloud to them. Much joy came to Ellen through books.

It was Phyllis who first introduced Ellen to Dr. Seuss, but Ellen was not beyond devouring him on her own.

She would go to the public library in Greenville, mount the old wooden backstairs to the children's room, and beeline her way to the shelf of Dr. Seuss books. Knowing the limits the librarian would impose on her enthusiasm, Ellen would carefully count out three books to take home.

Eventually, of course, even with repeated readings, she ran out of Dr. Seuss books. So Phyllis began writing new ones for her.

Phyllis not only concocted her own nonsensical verses, she filled the pages with her own Dr. Seuss-inspired illustrations. She invented some thoroughly weird and delightful creatures to entertain her daughter and to increase Ellen's capacity to read. Phyllis's choice of vocabulary held nothing back in deference to Ellen's age. Ellen was challenged to read what Phyllis had written.

It was her mother's example that taught Ellen that ordinary people could write books, even ordinary people like her.

Why not?

So Ellen began her first book and called it *Chinaberry*. Where the title came from is anybody's guess, but *Chinaberry* is what she chose. It was also her lead character's name.

Chinaberry, a black boy about Ellen's age, owned a spotted dog. The dog answered to the highly original name of Spot.

Chinaberry wanted to enter Spot in a dog show but was turned away because Spot was not an American Kennel Club-certified purebred. Ellen knew about the AKC and its special breeds; her family owned one.

Alas, Chinaberry's Spot was nothing more than a mutt, a mongrel.

So Chinaberry put flour on Spot's spots, and somehow (through logic only an author could accept) this quite obvious ruse fooled the judges into letting Spot into the dog show. Once there, Spot's warm and friendly personality won the judges' hearts, and Chinaberry was awarded a big medal on a blue ribbon to hang around Spot's neck.

At this point, Spot ran through water, which washed off the flour. Instantly the judges recognized Spot for the mutt he was. But instead of being upset, they complimented themselves on their wisdom. They had been smart enough to make a good and right decision.

Congratulatory handshakes all around ended the book.

A happily-ever-after ending is exactly what Ellen, a young schoolgirl whose sense of justice was pricked daily, wanted imposed on the segregated world she saw around her. It didn't take any genius to see what her story was saying.

After finishing the story, Ellen took it to her mother. Phyllis read it aloud and then told Ellen she had done something important. She encouraged Ellen to illustrate her book, and so she did.

Ellen's pictures of Chinaberry and Spot and the judges and all the other beautiful but non-winning dogs decorated the pages and margins of her book. Then Phyllis bound it for her in a neat yellow cardboard cover and they kept it for many, many years.

Thinking Deeply

Is there anything we want more for our children than for them to learn how to think?

Thinking is education's ultimate prize.

But it's not a prize *schools* give out too regularly.

It's not that schools are bad, though of course some are. It's that they are geared toward *mass* education—that is, education of the masses. Some individual attention is available in schools. but not very much.

Now, I'm a believer in public education. In fact, I'm a strong believer in public education. I detail my beliefs about how to merge Christianity and public education in my book *Who Will Be My Teacher?* Public schools help create a literate populace, pass on cultural norms, convey a sense of historical perspective. They help unify us as a people. They give us common ground and help make us glad we share it.

But how can we tell schools (meaning, school*teachers*) to be mommies and daddies and religious leaders and nurses and social workers and developmental psychologists and hygienists and nutritionists and sex educators and cops and everything else we unceasingly demand of them and STILL expect them to teach ALL kids to think and reason and read and write?

We parents must recognize our central role in our children's educational life no matter where or under what circumstances our children attend school, be it public, private, or home.

No curriculum can replace us. None.

Education doesn't start with school, and it doesn't end there either. It's a lifelong process.

And thinking is the crux of it. Thinking is education's heart, its core, its *raison d'être.*

Phyllis did so many things right in the story above. Let's enumerate some of them.

First, she showed her children that while one set of standards existed in other homes, her home was different. Racial segregation was not allowed in the place where she ruled the roost.

Second, she gave her children outlets for their questions and feelings. She gave them the gift of her time and she gave them the gift of literacy. She helped them love words and see the power of both written and oral language.

Third, she encouraged them to write by writing herself. Moreover, she bound *their* writings into real books that they could keep and reread, just like any other real book.

Fourth, she helped them deal with the large issues of life, those imponderables worth our poor attempts at pondering.

It's essential that we teach our kids to think. Modeling and talking, practicing and preaching, are two powerful teaching tools, perhaps the most powerful.

I hold strong anti-abortion sentiments. In my state, *Roe v. Wade* has been interpreted more broadly than in some other states. Third trimester abortions are performed regularly—clear through the ninth month of pregnancy. I'm appalled that we not only have a federal law upholding this practice, but that we dispense public monies to support it.

Fred and I have never hidden our feelings about this tragedy from our children. Together we study the abortion position of national and local political candidates. Together we discover whose position most nearly resembles ours.

Our habits include regularly following political candidates. In our house, we watch debates, track issues, tirelessly discuss the merits of various viewpoints, examine advertising practices, search for slickness and shallowness, match rhetoric to record.

Even now, with Marc a couple of thousand miles away at school, he'll call home after a nationally televised debate to discuss it with us, simply for the adrenal high. Quite simply, we love to talk politics with each other.

Neither Fred nor I tell our kids how to think, what decisions to make. Instead, we demonstrate the process *we* go through.

What are some ways parents can help their kids learn how to think? I believe all TV shows are ripe with teachable moments. We can use TV for our purposes rather than allowing it to use us.

By its nature, television is passive. We don't interact with what we see. We sit back and let it happen to us.

When we glue ourselves to the tube, our brains are put on hold, they're numbed, prevented from doing much thinking.

Is the answer banning TV from our homes?

Not in my opinion.

The answer, in my opinion, is teaching our children how to deal with television, how to discriminate and bring intelligence to it, how to rise above its pervasive influence.

As someone who has spent nearly half her professional life around television studios, I urge you to watch television with your kids.

Whatever interests children, we should be watching too, even if it's a soap opera or game show, as disgusting or silly as those programs may be to us. Putting television into the hands of unattended children is not unlike tossing a book of matches at them as they head out the door to play. Nothing's inherently wrong with fire, but proper use requires structure.

Our presence on the couch next to our children is very important. Only a live presence—*ours*—can turn TV into an active learning experience. Only a live presence can jog kids' minds into gear.

Why shouldn't children believe everything they see if we do nothing to prevent it? Does taking television away from them prevent it? What happens when they spend time at their friend's house or when they hear about TV shows on the school playground?

We should be there to discuss what we see, to sort out our family's values from those represented on TV. We should zero in on subliminal messages, on nonverbal cues, on the media's manipulation of us. We should help our children *think* about everything TV teaches, about everything it shows, about why programmers program as they do.

Just as I don't believe children can or should be shielded from television's cafeteria of junk, I also don't believe children should be shielded from tragedy, from life and death issues, from their own and their parents' mortality, from the pain of dealing with difficult life transitions.

Take death, for instance. Death is part of life. Death is inevitable. Children must encounter death in order to understand it. They should attend funerals. They should have an opportunity to gaze at the waxen, lifeless bodies of people they once knew as alive and vibrant.

Pets often offer very young children their first encounter with what it means to die.

One day Jason's goldfish died. Jason wasn't particularly alarmed. Instead, he waited patiently for his father to come home and fix it. Didn't Daddy always fix his broken toys? As far as Jason could tell, this was more of the same.

But of course it wasn't more of the same. The day his goldfish died was the day Jason discovered his daddy wasn't God.

It was an important discovery. Jason saw death firsthand and learned that some things in life are both inevitable and irrevocable. By being human, by being incapable of resurrecting a goldfish, Jason's father eased his son toward larger learnings.

Good teachers reach out to children during specific pinpricks of time and capitalize on teachable moments. Parents have at least eighteen years of daily contact with kids. God has given us the time and the opportunity to guide our children toward an understanding of how to think deeply.

When children learn to think, they gain protection against false or poor teaching. They learn to ask questions, to test answers. They learn to assume responsibility for themselves, for the choices they make.

Just as importantly, they learn to make those choices. Children who head down life's rutty paths and who ask hard questions about all that they see and experience sometimes become nettled, even unsatisfied, with the answers they find. But that's all right.

In fact, *it's the way it should be.*

Everyone needs to discover that ready answers never were education's prize. Education's prize has always been found in learning to think.

Questions for each of us to ask ourselves:

—How much thinking do I do? Do I ever carefully examine my opinions? Am I uncomfortable living with questions, with those things I don't know how to answer?

—When my children question me, what's my response? To give them a quick answer? Or to help them discover more about how to find answers for themselves?

—Is television a frequent babysitter in my home? How can I use it more intelligently?

—Do I regularly discuss serious issues with my children? Do I discuss politics with them? Life and death? War and peace? Sex? Justice? The environment? Responsibility to others? What's one topic my children and I could discuss this week? How could I introduce it?

CHAPTER 11

"The Mom Who Spawned a Travelogue"

KIMBERLY'S mother had always read to her. Even before she could talk, Kim would sit on her mother's lap and page through illustrated books and magazines, her mother pointing out the objects in each picture and calling them by name. Soon they progressed from this early stepping-stone to books with stories. Kimberly learned from an early age to love books.

It was not surprising, then, that she taught herself to read while sitting on her mother's lap.

At least, it was certain no one else did it. No one ever formally taught Kim any reading principles or phonetic pronunciations. The fact was, Kim could read before she started school.

Even after Kim could read for herself, her mother continued their read-aloud tradition. But then, after Kim learned how to talk, her mother continued *talking* to her, didn't she? Why should reading be any different?

Kim's mother knew that something important was being shared when she and Kim read together and that nothing could ever substitute for it, not even Kim's serendipitous reading independence.

They had two favorite read-aloud times. The first was every night before bed. The second was during family trips in the car.

Time passed quickly on long car rides. While Kim's father would drive, Kim's mother would read. Sometimes Kim's father would get so engrossed in the story that, even while the car was hurtling down the highway, he'd crane his neck to see if there were any pictures.

Kim's mother told him to do his job—drive safely—and she'd do hers—make certain he got to see any and all pictures at some appropriate future stop along the road.

Kim's mother was named Lucille. Kim's father was named George. George and Lucille may sound like names for two stodgy, staid, old fogeys but someone forgot to tell that to George and Lucille. These two exercised creative teaching skills as easily as they breathed.

When Kim was younger, they read wonderful stories together: *The Elephant's Child, Sylvester and the Magic Pebble, Ira Sleeps Over, Charlotte's Web, James and the Giant Peach,* and all the *Ramona* books.

When she was older, they wept over *Where the Red Fern Grows* and *The Yearling;* explored the theological implications of *Tuck Everlasting, A Wrinkle in Time,* and *The Lion, the Witch, and the Wardrobe;* by turns laughed and thrilled to *The Princess Bride;* and endlessly discussed the issue of moral courage raised in *To Kill a Mockingbird.*

One evening Lucille began reading *Little House in the Big Woods* aloud. Almost immediately Kim was caught. She wanted to read each one of the *Little House* books, and so she did.

The Ingalls family—their daily lives, their tragedies, triumphs, and homely celebrations—transported Kim back in time. From what Lucille and George could see, Kim might have herself become the spritely Laura Ingalls of a hundred years earlier, a thoughtful, aware girl destined to marry Almanzo Wilder and live to a durable old age.

"What would you think," Lucille asked one day, "about taking a trip this summer as if *we* were the Ingalls family? How would you like to travel to all the places they lived, to follow in their tracks, so to speak?"

"Could we?" Kim asked hopefully.

George smiled his approval. "Why didn't I think of that?" he asked, tenderly patting his wife's bottom. "I make a mighty good Pa, you know."

And so the planning began. The three of them got out a United States atlas and coordinated each of the Wilder books with a location on the map. They wanted to make a chronological loop, to trace Laura Ingalls Wilder's life in the order Laura herself had lived it.

Their travels would take them through parts of Wisconsin, Minnesota, South Dakota, Iowa, Kansas, Missouri, and even, for one far-reaching stop on the Ingalls family journey, clear to the Eastern Seaboard.

They carefully plotted the number of miles between locations and computed how much distance they could expect to cover in a day. They matched the Ingalls family's moves as accurately as possible with modern highways and current geographical realities.

And they also ran some mathematical comparisons of how long it would have taken the Ingalls family to get from place to place, considering they were traveling by wagon, not car.

George and Lucille involved Kimberly in every bit of the trip's planning. She was called upon to make computations and calculations, to glean information from books and then apply what she'd learned to the dilemma at hand—tracing Laura's lifelong route in the two summer weeks available to George and Lucille as vacation from their jobs.

Kim's homework (literal and true *home*work) ranged from arithmetic and research skills to reading and writing to American history, social studies, and geography.

The trip proposed by Lucille and enthusiastically endorsed by the other two turned out to be the wonderful and memorable implementation of an entire academic curriculum . . . knowledge enrichment of the highest degree.

Everything held relevance and meaning for Kim. Lucille, George, and Laura Ingalls Wilder's own books were Kim's resources, her teachers. They helped Kim learn how to solve problems independently, how to learn outside the formal walls of a classroom.

Establishing Knowledge

My, how many possibilities there are here for parents! The problem is not in finding enough ideas, but in finding enough time to implement them. Suddenly the years our children live in our homes seem few indeed.

Recently I spent an entire spring semester teaching English at a women's college in Pusan, South Korea. I went by myself without family, without friends, without any English-speaking companions. I was completely *alone*. What I knew about Korean people and Korean customs would barely have registered on the seismograph of available Western knowledge.

Believe me, when I came back to the States and asked the customs agent in Honolulu to greet me with a "Welcome home!", I was no longer ignorant.

By then, I felt nearly half-Korean. I left many dear friends in Korea. In fact, I knew so many people so well I wept at having to bid them good-bye. I also brought back a mental file full of facts and information.

A few years later, I still haven't shaken the feeling of being part-Korean. A part of me continues to live in Korea.

It's the strangest thing.

But it has a lot to do with what this chapter's all about: *establishing knowledge.*

Those thirteen weeks were glorious and strengthening and difficult. I could say a lot about my semester-long sojourn to Korea, but I won't . . . except for this one thing: I went over as the teacher and came home as the one taught.

No doubt I contributed an English word or two to my students' linguistic repertoire. But whatever knowledge I passed on, nothing compared to what I received.

Or should I say consented to receive? After all, I (the learner) had to be receptive. I had to open myself up. I had to make myself vulnerable, even defenseless.

Any one of us can refuse to allow in outside stimuli. We can wall ourselves off and close ourselves down. We can rest on self-righteousness or indignation or loneliness or self-sufficiency or whatever we want to rest on. We can even rest on our laurels.

But then, of course, we won't develop, won't grow, won't learn anything new.

At times, Korea felt very unfair to me, and I felt very selfish. I was the one commissioned to teach. I was (particularly in Korean terms) the well-salaried professor.

Yet it was not my students who were gaining the most; it was *I.* Although I was there to contribute to their lives, the Korean people gave far more to me than I could ever hope to give back.

And I was greedy to take it. I wanted to learn, remember, smell, taste, eat up this strange new country that soon seemed less strange, more familiar, even beloved.

Many others do things like this; I don't pretend to be unique. All you have to do is look around to see how any number of parents work at increasing their own, as well as their children's, world knowledge.

Families take trips to visit Civil War battlefields to learn firsthand about that important chapter of our country's history, to grapple on location with the issue of slavery and with the paradox of violent death in pastoral surroundings.

They take trips to Arizona and North Carolina to observe the sophisticated cultures of Native Americans—Navajo, Cherokee, Ute—as well as to better understand both historical and current tragedies.

They take trips to Pennsylvania's Amish country, or to the orthodox Jewish neighborhoods of Chicago or New York, or to San Francisco's Chinatown, all to get a flavor of other religions, other cultures, other ways of living.

Families interested in establishing knowledge in their homes contrast the borders of Mexico with the borders of Canada, the woods of Wisconsin with the flats of Nevada, the cities of the two coasts with the farmlands of the Midwest.

They tour Washington, D.C., or their state capital. They sit in on a session of Congress or the legislature or a criminal court case.

They visit zoos and libraries and museums. They go to plays and movies.

They balance quick trips to fast food outlets with occasional leisurely dinners at a nice restaurant replete with white tablecloths and linen napkins. They sample authentic Vietnamese or Cajun or Afghan (yes, Afghan!) cooking.

They take in sporting events from the familiar football and basketball to the exotic lacrosse and fencing.

They share a variety of musical experiences, everything from opera to jazz to rock, including representative smatterings of both vocal and instrumental artists.

I even know a family of six that uproots itself now and then to live in locations like Africa and Samoa for anything from a few weeks to a year. Everybody willingly packs up and participates in these work adventures, then comes back to talk about their experiences as casually and naturally as if they never left their middle class Colorado town.

Interactive learning is so important, it mustn't be overlooked. It's essential. It's key. Parents who care about establishing knowledge in their homes give their children and themselves a smorgasbord of hands-on experiences with the world beyond their doors.

And they back everything up by having good reference books available and ready to use in their homes— basic things like an atlas, a set of encyclopedia, a dictionary and thesaurus, an almanac, perhaps even a computer.

But just as importantly, they invest in materials that intrigue members of the family, materials relating to the Titanic or the Holocaust, to automobile repair or baseball statistics or, yes, to Laura Ingalls Wilder's frontier life.

All of us travel vicariously through time and space via books and other materials and are far, far richer for it. So what's the moral to my story? Just this: Lots and lots of reference material, research material—an accumulation of *knowledge*—should be available in the middle of our living rooms.

But that's not the end of it. The next step is for us to talk, talk, talk about everything with our children. You name it, we should explore it—*and* we should talk about it. It's imperative that we fill our homes with talk.

Talking helps our children crystallize their values. It helps them understand the experiences we've shared. It helps them pull out what's troubling, interesting, awesome, frightening, or simply fun about those experiences.

A simple conversation after a rock concert could begin like this: "What did you think when those drums started rolling on that last piece? When it started soft and then kept getting louder and louder?"

"I liked it," our child might reply.

"Yeah, me too," we say back. "I felt it sort of pounding through me, like it was in my own stomach or something, and I started getting excited, you know, kind of tense and watchful, wondering what was coming next."

"You did? Me too. Yeah, that's how I felt too."

"It was pretty neat, wasn't it? But I have to say, I'm glad it didn't go on too long. I think I might've gotten tired of it if the composer had overdone it."

"Yeah," our child agrees. "Me too." And why wouldn't our child be inclined to agree? After all, we haven't judged taste; we've only expressed a reasoned opinion.

By demonstrating acceptance of something our child likes, and by liking parts of it ourselves, we've made it possible for our opinion to be heard. We've done it in a way that allows our son or daughter at some point down the road to be more fair with something, or with someone, that he or she might not particularly like.

But we shouldn't stop there.

"How do people write that kind of music, do you suppose?" we might go on to ask. "How do they learn to do it?"

Our child, who by now is getting into the spirit of this conversation, may suggest, "Maybe they first sound it out on a piano. You know, maybe they kind of play around with some tunes on the keys."

"Maybe they do," we reply. "Boy, I wish I could do that! I've often wished I could play the piano better than I do. I've often wished I hadn't quit taking piano lessons. I used to give my mother such a hard time about it. What a little pain I was!"

It's possible, of course, that we could lead our child into a new or renewed interest in piano lessons. Strange, wonderful things *do* happen when we make a commitment to talk with our kids just as if they are—dare I say it?—real people.

There are many, many things we can talk about, and teach, after a shared experience like a concert. But before we can share the experience on a conversational level, we must already have shared it in reality.

They are lucky kids indeed whose parents know that the best first words they can teach are *LOOK AND LISTEN.*

Charles William Eliot, president of Harvard for forty years, attended a dinner held in his honor. Various Harvard professors vied with each other for the honor of proposing toasts to their president.

One congratulated him on achieving miracles at the university. "Since you became president," the speaker said, "Harvard has become a storehouse of knowledge."

Eliot avowed the compliment. "What you say is true," he responded, "but I can claim little credit for it. It is simply that the freshmen bring so much and the seniors take so little away."

We are the seniors in our homes, our children the freshmen. Heaven keep us from complacency!

We need to be learners with our children. We need to be co-adventurers along the Knowledge Acquisition Trail. We need to acquire eyes that see and ears that hear.

We have the responsibility, accompanied by the opportunity, to help our children understand that God loves all people, to realize that God, while certainly bigger than they or we can imagine, also takes special delight in forming the individual.

We have the responsibility, accompanied by the opportunity, to help our children appreciate that the world has many different ways of expressing itself, and that ours is one of those ways.

We have the responsibility, accompanied by the opportunity, to help our children be comfortable in several different settings and at home in ours, to seal them within shared humanity, to bond them to this planet's other inhabitants, to let them sup at the tables of the world.

We have the responsibility, accompanied by the opportunity, to help our children—most wonderful of all!—satisfy their priceless, precious, God-given curiosity.

Questions for each of us to ask ourselves:
   —Do I actively encourage development of my children's interests?

—Do I consciously seek to help my children appreciate other cultures? Other ways of living? Diverse types of people?

—What kind of role model am I? Do I show by personal example that reading and writing are important to life?

—Have I made myself aware of the many learning opportunities available to my family within my own community?

CHAPTER 12

"The Teen Who Longed for a Car"

V INCE was a bright high school student who had struggled with his grades ever since sixth grade. He put little time or energy into thoughts of school and, if it was possible, even less into completing his homework.

What saved Vince from academic oblivion was his enormous retentive capacity. He could pass tests because he remembered nearly everything said during class. His teachers' lectures stuck with him. Every word of them.

Vince's peculiar ability allowed him to make an occasional *B* without effort. *C*s were a cinch.

Except perhaps for English, where Vince was required to do a considerable amount of reading and writing *outside* of class. Outside assignments figured prominently enough into his total grade that, in English at least, Vince often hovered between a *D* and an *F*.

Vince's parents had very little idea how to help him. They had tried threats and punishments; they had withheld privileges; they had grounded him. They had taken away television, the telephone, his allowance.

That wasn't all. They had appealed to his intelligence ("Don't you want people to know how smart you are?"), to his concern for his future ("What if you want to go to a good college?"), to his pride ("Wouldn't you like to see your name on the honor roll?"), and even to his greed ("We'll pay you for each *A* you make.")

In their desperation they were willing to try almost anything.

Nothing they had ever tried had motivated Vince to improve his grades. He slogged on through school just like he always had.

But when it came time for their son to drive, when he turned sixteen, Vince's parents, Owen and Sylvia, looked at each other knowingly. They were certain they had finally found the answer to their dilemma.

Vince very much wanted to be able to drive. It seemed like getting his license and being able to drive was his main—perhaps only—goal in life.

So Vince's parents, who never let an opportunity go by if they could help it, told Vince that if he got an *A* in Drivers' Education, he could drive their second car to school each day.

Lo and behold, after the course was finished, Vince came home with a *B*. He had never cracked a book, never opened a manual.

He also didn't get the car.

"What happened?" his frustrated parents chorused. "Why did you get just a *B*?"

Vince shrugged. "You're going to punish me for getting a *B*?" he asked. "I get a *B* and that's not good enough for you?"

"We had a bargain: No *A*, no car. Remember? We're just keeping our end of the bargain. That's not the same as punishing you."

"You're punishing me, all right," Vince insisted. "You won't let me have the car because you want to punish me for not getting one of your beloved *A*s."

"Wrong," his father said.

"Wrong," his mother said.

"It would be a punishment if it was your right to drive," said Owen. "It's not a right in this family; driving to school is a privilege, not a right. Other parents may treat it like a right. We don't."

"We were going to *reward* you for getting an *A*," Sylvia clarified. "That's very different from punishing you for not getting one. We don't see them as having an either/or relationship. It's not always a 'one or the other' world, Vincent. By offering you the car, we were going to let you do something that you wouldn't normally have gotten to do."

"But you didn't get the *A*," Owen pointed out, "so we're back to what's normal in this house. And no car for you to drive to school is what's normal in this house."

Unconvinced, Vince kept calling it a punishment for the next several weeks.

But his parents did not back down. Despite the pressure Vince applied, despite what some might even say was emotional blackmail—after all, his parents would have greatly appreciated less stress and more smiles, as Vince very well knew—they held firmly to their original bargain. You meet the terms that both parties agree to, or the agreement is null and void.

However, they were willing to negotiate new terms with Vince for the following semester.

"What do you think would be fair?" Owen asked his son one day. "Under what conditions would you like to see us reopen our offer to let you drive the car to school next semester? If you made straight *A*s?"

Vince made a face. "Give me a break," he said. "Straight *A*s? Be real!"

"Oh, you don't think you could make straight *A*s?"

"What if I could?" Vince asked. "The point is, I don't *want* to. Who gives a rip about straight *A*s, anyway?"

"Colleges."

"You mean," Vince said, aghast, "that Cronenwett Brothers Trash-Hauling School won't take me unless I make straight *A*s?"

"Well, it's at least a possibility," his father said with a smile. "So if not straight *A*s, what then? What do you think's fair? What's reasonable—I mean, that we *both* can agree to?"

"Straight *B*s?" Vince offered.

Owen thought that one over for a moment. "Straight *B*s would be an improvement," he said. "But driving the car is a pretty nice privilege, Vince. I think you'd go along with that, wouldn't you? That it's a pretty nice privilege? It's one I'd like to've had. I never got to drive to school when I was your age. We're not talking about *rights,* remember; we're talking about *privileges.* Just because a lot of your friends do it doesn't make it a right."

"Yeah, yeah," Vince said, "so how about the honor roll? Suppose I made the honor roll. Would you let me drive the car then?"

The honor roll meant half *B*s and half *A*s.

"The honor roll's good," Owen said. "Yeah, I like the honor roll. I can live with the honor roll. Let me see if your mother can live with the honor roll."

She could. Happily.

A few weeks later, Vince came to them again. "If I brought home a note from each teacher saying I had straight *A*s right now, could I start driving the car to school?"

"You mean like right now? This very week?"

"Yeah, I mean like right now, this very week."

His parents looked at Vince, then at each other, then back at Vince. "Sure, okay," they said. "If your teachers tell us you have straight *A*s across the board this week, the car is yours starting now."

"But I don't have to keep straight *A*s until the end of the semester, right? The honor roll is still all right for that?"

Exhausted, they conceded this point. "Yes, the honor roll is still all right for that."

The very next night Vince brought home a letter signed by each of his six teachers. Vince had straight *A*s with just three weeks left in the semester. His parents were relieved—no, overjoyed.

In order to be listed on the honor roll, Vince had to make certain that no more than three of his *A*s dropped to *B*s.

When the semester was over, Vince came home with two *A*s and four *B*s. His *A*s were in P.E. and Music. His four major academic courses—Algebra, English, German, and Biology—had all drifted downward from *A*s to *B*s.

"Hey," Vince pointed out, correctly, "it's better than I've ever done before."

Owen and Sylvia studied his report card, not knowing the best way to respond. They were saddened and disappointed that more of the *A*s hadn't had staying power.

"We're very pleased with the overall improvement you've made," Owen acknowledged. "But it's still not what we agreed to, is it?"

"All you had to do was hang onto one more of those *A*s," Sylvia pointed out plaintively. "Just one more, that's all."

"So what about the car?" asked Vince, getting right to the heart of the matter.

"Well," Owen said by way of answer, "how about letting your mother and me talk? Go on to your room for a few minutes, okay?"

When they were alone, Vince's mother nearly collapsed. "We have to give him the car, Owen," she said. "We have to."

"Why do we have to?"

"Because he's done so much better."

"I don't want to discourage him anymore than you do, Sylvia. But he still didn't meet the standards all three of us agreed to. He fell short of them."

"Only a little."

"I know, only a little."

"What if he promises to make the honor roll next time? What if we let him drive, telling him that's a sign of our trust that he can do it next time, that we fully expect it of him, but that he more or less has to promise us he'll be on the honor roll next semester? Don't you think he'd respond positively to us putting our trust in him that completely? He wouldn't dare disappoint our trust, would he?"

"He has to do it for himself, Sylvia, not for us. He has to learn to accept responsibility for himself. This was his goal for himself. He set it himself. Is it right to reward him for not reaching a goal he himself set?"

"So it's no car then?" she asked.

"What do you think of telling him that yes, for now it's no car, but that as soon as he brings home a note from one of the classes he got a *B* in——as soon as he has one of his teachers tell us he's raised his grade in that class to an *A*—that he can then have the car immediately? That puts the timetable for getting the car back squarely in Vince's lap and no one else's."

"I just don't want him to get discouraged! I was so sure he would do it this time! He was so close! He had straight *A*s just a few weeks ago!"

There was nothing Owen could say. He felt the same way.

Later, when Sylvia went to Vince's room to talk to her son alone, she said, "What's the best thing for us to do, Vince? I really don't know what's right anymore. I *wanted* you to have that car to drive to school. I wanted it so badly for you! In fact, I just knew it was going to happen. I just *knew* it."

Goodness, she thought, *if you don't watch it, girl, you're going to cry right here and now.*

"So what do you want us to do now?" she asked. "Go ahead and give the car to you anyway? What do *you* think is right in this situation, Vincent?"

Evidently Vince saw his mother's anguish. He reached out gently and comfortingly to touch her arm. Then, looking her directly in the eye, he said in a quiet, adult voice, "Mom, it's all right. I haven't earned the car yet. But I will. Don't worry, I *am* going to be on the honor roll. You'll see."

Accepting Responsibility

None of us change until we take responsibility for ourselves. That's all there is to it.

We parents can agonize, threaten, wheedle, cajole, fret, fume, and foam at the mouth but our children ultimately make their own decisions; we can't do that for them. We can say all the right things, parent *perfectly,* and still our children may not respond the way we want them to.

I think you need to know that Vince did not make the honor roll the next semester. In fact, his grades slipped even lower.

The success Vince's parents scored was in making a distinction between rights and responsibilities. I believe it's a good, healthy distinction.

Just look around at society today. Have you ever seen such a tort-happy group of people? Lawsuits, lawsuits everywhere.

We spend so much time ballyhooing our sacred "rights" that almost no energy is devoted to recognizing our obligations, our responsibilities.

We have come a long way from the day when spines shivered and eyes grew fervent as John F. Kennedy's voice rang out, "Ask not what your country can do for you; ask what you can do for your country!"

Now campaigns are built around quite different slogans. Now political rallying cries go something along the order of, "You're not getting enough of what's due you? By golly, stick with me; I'll make 'em cough it up!"

What a lesson in dependency that is!

Responsibility, on the other hand, is liberating. It allows us to control what happens to us. We don't turn that control over to someone else. And we accept the consequences, good and bad, of our choices.

Where their actions are concerned, our children are the ones who reap the rewards of their behavior and, of course, suffer the consequences for it.

To develop a sense of responsibility, kids must *have* responsibility. Kids learn to care for themselves and about others by performing caring actions. This means taking responsibility for themselves—their bodies, their possessions, their rooms, their homework, their spending money.

But it also means taking other-oriented responsibilities—caring for pets or for younger brothers and sisters; shoveling snow for an elderly neighbor; helping out at home with chores that normally fall to Mom or Dad, chores like kitchen cleanup, lawn mowing, car washing.

When I was nine, I was ill enough to be flat on my back for nearly five months. My parents gave me a parakeet for companionship. Eventually I wound up with two parakeets: Zeke and Zack. I tamed them, taught them to talk, and incessantly played with them. I also was in charge of their care and feeding. Sometimes my mother reminded me to clean their cage, but she never did it for me. The birds were my responsibility.

Certain household tasks can be earmarked especially for children. These can become regular, ongoing assignments.

In our home, Kyle is the macaroni and cheese chef. No one cooks it the way he does. In particular, he complains that we don't know the right amount of milk to add, that our amateur efforts create less than a satisfactory finished product. As the expert in our family, he's probably right. I know it's tasty when he does it.

In other homes, one child is responsible for baking brownies. In still others, one child sculpts the front hedge or prunes the roses.

In the child's designated area, he or she is the leader, the one the rest of the family looks to. Pride in accomplishment is important for developing a sense of responsibility.

When Marc was six years old he planted a pumpkin patch. It swallowed a huge portion of our backyard. Marc watered his pumpkins, oversaw their care, and when they were ripe, peddled them throughout the neighborhood from the back of his red wagon.

One elderly widow rewarded Marc by taking the pumpkin she'd bought from him and making it into a pie. She then invited Marc and our family over to eat it with her. Never has Marc enjoyed pumpkin pie more than he did that day!

Knowing that something good happens because of them helps commit our children to ever-widening circles of responsibility.

As parents we provide excellent models of responsibility to children when we apologize to them for our own inappropriate actions. At these healthy "I'm sorry" moments, our kids don't see us blaming others; they see us accepting personal responsibility for what we do and say.

By accepting responsibility for ourselves, we give up the yoke of victimhood and take on the yoke of servanthood. Responsibility frees us.

I covet that freedom for myself; I also covet it for my children.

Besides, why put ourselves through the agony that Owen and Sylvia did? We're incapable of altering our children's behavior. We can't *make* them do anything.

If our kids don't take responsibility for themselves, *our* taking it won't accomplish much. They are the ones, through the empowerment of the Holy Spirit, who can change themselves. We're not. Change happens from the inside out, not from the outside in.

We can't assume command over our children's lives, no matter how hard we try. No matter what we do (especially when we're trying extra hard to do "It" right, to find that "One Trick That Always Works"), our children are apt to go their own merry ways.

They are independent, autonomous creatures, our kids. And so, in the end, all we can do as parents is build a house of love, supported by word and deed, whose foundation rests squarely on solid instruction and faith in God. We can construct a home environment that invites our children to assume leadership over their own lives.

That's a difficult task, of course. But far from an impossible one.

Questions for each of us to ask ourselves:
—Do my children know the difference between rights and responsibilities? Do they know why it's important to recognize that there is a difference? Do I?

—What home responsibilities do I allow my children to have? Are they really in charge of those things? How do I reward them for taking charge?

—Am I feeling pressure to be a perfect parent? What exactly do I think a perfect parent is?

—Can I relax and enjoy my kids more? What's one thing I could do right now to begin that process?

IV

KIDS
WITH
FAITH

CHAPTER 13

"The Parents Who Prayed without Ceasing"

SOME of the stories I've written in this book are my own. I, for instance, was the young shoplifter in the dime store. I was also the girl who grew up in a family that bonded itself through traditions, traditions Fred and I continue.

And I was the one who groped to understand the pre-integrated South, the child who penned a little tome called *Chinaberry*.

This next story is mine, too. It's important that you know that going in. I warn you, it's an intensely personal story.

It's also the most amazing story I've ever lived. Nothing else comes close. It's how I learned that God loves my children even more than I do.

Simple? Self-evident?

Not to me.

As I write this, our son Marc is twenty-one years old. From the time he was twelve, all he ever wanted to be was a West Point cadet.

Initially, I was anything but supportive of Marc's desire. I even counseled him against it. Most of my concern centered in Marc himself. Marc is a bright nonconformist. In many ways, he's a maverick. He has the soul of a poet and the perspective of an artist.

I was troubled. Marc's personality didn't fit my image of the military. How could Marc be a person God intended for military discipline and structure? I simply couldn't see it, couldn't accept it. Certainly Marc had enough talents (artistic, athletic, academic) to give him many future options. God could easily divert him into any number of other career choices.

Or so I reasoned.

But Marc never deviated from his desire to be a West Point cadet. Never. Not even once.

My cousin's husband is a dentist. He told Marc that he had a patient who was a West Point graduate. A meeting was arranged between Marc and a retired colonel named Bill. It was the odd birth of an important relationship.

After telling us that Marc was the best prospective cadet he'd ever seen, Bill determined early on—perhaps before that fateful first meeting was over—to help Marc in any way he could. He outlined an ideal high school plan that would strongly support Marc's future West Point candidacy.

But Marc suffered many defeats, some of them self-inflicted. Ultimately (or so it seemed at the time) Marc's West Point dreams came down to an election for student body president. He could compensate, on the West Point pre-candidate tally system, for many of his previous defeats by being elected president of his student body.

Marc ran one of the most imaginative and humorous campaigns I have ever seen, and I've been around school elections most of my life. But the assistant principal, far from being amused by it, blasted Marc for "cheating."

Marc invented comical new campaign devices, things that had never been done. According to this principal's logic, Marc's creativity gave him an "unfair advantage" over his opponents.

I feared greatly that Marc wouldn't win, *couldn't* win. In particular, my fear focused on what would happen to *Marc* if he didn't win. So much of his future dream seemed directly tied to the success of this election!

On the day of the election, I said this prayer: "Lord, you are going to have to do something. I can do nothing for Marc; only you can. You know what is riding on `this election. You could have chosen to divert Marc from his goal during the last five years, but for whatever reason, you never did. So, Lord, I leave this election in your hands. It's all up to you now."

Then I left the empty library classroom I was sitting in at Friends University. The classroom door **led** directly to the children's literature book collection.

As I walked by those shelves of familiar books, preoccupied with my thoughts of Marc and the election even then taking place, a new title seemed to leap out at me, stopping me in my tracks.

MIRACLES, it said.

I took the book into my hand and examined it more closely. It was a collection of poems written by children.

What was I to make of this? That God was trying to communicate with me?

I was convinced he was; I still am.

I fully believe that at that moment, in direct response to my prayer, God promised me a miracle.

But I was wrong about which miracle it was. Actually, I would continue to be wrong many times more.

At that moment, however, I was utterly happy and sure. Marc had won the election! Despite the assistant principal, he'd won! I just knew it.

"Thank you, Lord!" I remember saying aloud.

Marc called my office a couple of hours later. His voice was quiet and subdued. He told me he'd lost, but I refused to believe him. I knew he'd won. I *knew* it. I told him to quit joking, that of course he'd won.

When he repeated that he'd lost, I still refused to believe him.

"Mom," he said, his tone stony, "if you tell me one more time that I won, I'm going to hang up on you. I did *not* win. I *lost*. What is it that you can't understand?"

As it turned out, in a school of approximately twelve hundred students, Marc had lost the election by twenty votes.

My anguish and confusion were acute. Seeking help in dealing with this unexpected reality, I went to a theologian friend who gave me these wise, reassuring words: "Marti," he said, "if you're sure the 'miracles' episode is of God, then what you've been promised hasn't happened yet."

Though his prospects now were dimmer, Marc's desire to be a West Point cadet never wavered. Never. He pursued the Congressional nomination required and, in fact, received nominations not only to West Point but to Annapolis as well.

All of his paperwork was in order, including good results on his physical aptitude exam.

The only thing we hadn't heard about was Marc's medical evaluation. But Marc had always been healthy, always been athletic. He was in terrific physical shape.

While we were waiting anxiously for news of Marc's hoped-for admission to West Point, a bombshell dropped.

Marc's electrocardiogram showed an abnormality. The army, of course, wanted to learn the cause of the abnormality (needless to say, so did we). A cardiologist would need to do a full work-up on Marc before his West Point candidacy could be further considered.

We made the doctor's appointment, and Marc went through a day of extensive cardiac testing.

Finally, the week before Marc's final application papers were due at West Point, we got the cardiologist's report—one of those good news/bad news things.

The bad news was that Marc had a right bundle branch block, meaning that one of the three electrical circuits on the right side of his heart wasn't functioning. No signals were traveling along one of the three nerve routes designed to stimulate the right side of Marc's heart.

The good news was that he didn't need that circuit. The cardiologist's exact words were, "God gave us three times as many conduction systems as we need. All any of us requires is one working circuit, and Marc has two."

This blockage was not caused by disease; it was congenital. Marc had been born with it.

Because Marc was free of heart disease, the cardiologist assured us there was no reason why he couldn't participate in rigorous physical activity, that he was in no way impaired, that his condition posed no threat to his health and well-being at West Point or anywhere else.

But how West Point authorities would view this when they had thousands of "perfect" candidates was anybody's guess.

Unsurprisingly, Marc was devastated.

What particularly frightened me was Marc's anger at God. He saw his condition as evidence that God had a wicked sense of humor.

This was something *congenital*, after all. God had known it was there all along, from Marc's birth, even if the rest of us hadn't.

And what did God do with this privileged bit of knowledge, this inside information?

He had taken it right up to the end, then revealed it—from Marc's perspective—with a sort of "Gotcha!" smirk. To Marc, it was as if God were saying, "So you've wanted to go to West Point all these years? So it's all you've ever wanted? Well, guess what, kiddo—I'm saving the last laugh for me!"

This whole awful scenario seemed like evidence to Marc that God was either cruel or didn't exist at all. For the first time since he was a small boy, my son, now eighteen years old, allowed himself to sob in my arms.

I couldn't bear the loss of his dreams. Even more, I couldn't bear his hatred of God.

So, with Fred's help, I started praying that God would turn this nightmare into an opportunity for Marc, that God would finally deliver on the "miracles" promise I'd been given months before.

Specifically, Fred and I prayed that God would grant Marc early admission to West Point, that the unexpected diagnosis of a heart abnormality would be used to show Marc that God was sufficient in all things, that you didn't need "perfection" if you had God.

Fred and I have a prayer log. We write prayers on one side and answers—as we discern them—on the other. On December 5, 1985, we entered these words into our log:

> This is a special prayer, a prayer unlike any we have ever prayed before. We feel emboldened to come to you with this prayer, God, because of Marc's history and because we know you have been there in Marc's history at every step of the way. In April you promised Marti 'miracles' for Marc. We claim that promise, now. Never has a miracle been more needed for Marc's spiritual, emotional, and mental well-being.

> We specifically request early admission to West Point for Marc. Lord, please make this a Christmas present for Marc. And let a *major part* of the miracle be that Marc will know exactly who has been with him in all this, who it is that gives him this gift.

> We leave this in your hands. We ask you to fill the West Point admission officer's head with thoughts of Marc. We lay this supplication on Marc's behalf at your feet and praise you for your nurturing of our son. Thank you, in Christ's name.

We prayed the same prayer day after day, many times a day. As time went by and there was no word from West Point, we placed additional prayers in our log. One was capped by these words from the twenty-fourth verse of the ninth chapter of Mark: *Lord, I believe; help Thou my unbelief.*

> We pray that our faith will strengthen and not waver, that doubts and weakness will not be allowed to contaminate our focus on God's promises. We love you, Lord, and praise you for your goodness. May our faith and excitement grow stronger every day as we wait for your glorious fulfillment of the 'miracles' promise.

And still another prayer:

> Forgive our lack of adequacy in knowing precisely how to pray, Lord. But we know you know our hearts. You can see our hearts, you know our motivations, and we know that what is behind our prayer is your will: Marc's spiritual development, his quest to become a completed human being. Thank you for loving him and for hearing us. We commit all to you.

Finally, this prayer took its place alongside our daily litany:

> Lord, if you choose to use Bill [the colonel/ mentor we met at my cousin's house] as your human instrument in helping Marc get to West Point, please also help Marc see that you are behind it all, that Bill has been one example of your loving hand in his life.

That was the last prayer I recorded on this subject. The next several prayers in the log, many of which concerned other family issues, as well as this one, are in Fred's hand. It would be weeks before I entered another prayer. Christmas would come and go. A new year would begin.

And I would travel from the heights to the depths, catapulting myself emotionally from spiritual glory to darkest despair.

There was no miracle. At least not in terms *I* understood.

It is time for me to take you to a quiet December evening when I was doing nothing more extraordinary than stirring cream sauce at the stove.

That night—with Marc napping on the couch in the family room, with Fred recovering from a headache in our darkened bedroom, with Kyle quietly engaged in some private task upstairs—that night, with my family tucked securely around me, I felt a deep, quiet joy.

I came to sit beside Marc and, putting my hand on his head, began to pray.

I thanked God for his goodness, for his constancy in my life, for all the guides and teachers he'd provided me: my grandparents and parents, Fred and my sons, my friends Nancy and Bud and Vivian. My words of worship spanned all lobes of my conscious mind. I overflowed with love and adoration, emptying myself of everything but desire for God.

And in that emptying, Jesus Christ filled me. He filled me with his presence.

Somehow, from Somewhere, Jesus stood there in my family room with me. Improbable as it sounds, I not only felt his loving power, I *saw* it. Though it was dark outside, he was illuminated—silhouetted—against the window behind him. I couldn't see his face, but I had no trouble knowing Who it was. I recognized him instantly.

He lifted his arms, reaching them out as if to embrace me. Waves of warmth emanated from him and caught me in their glow, holding me transfixed.

God gave me a wonderful and unexpected gift that December night—a brief shining moment in the beam of absolute love. Love physically streamed toward me. Profound, unexplainable love.

Pure, holy, abundant love.

It was a serendipitous moment—not mine to create, only mine to receive.

My hand never left Marc's head, and my eyes never closed. I was wide-eyed and attentive the whole time. Two things, in retrospect, surprise me.

One is that Marc did not wake up, that he napped on, unperturbed by—indeed, unaware of—the almost electric power coursing through the room we shared. The other is that I felt no amazement at suddenly finding myself in the presence of my Lord. While I remained where I was, I did not stay there because I was somehow shocked into immobility.

On the contrary, it felt natural and right to have Jesus standing near me. It was, instead, almost like I was saying, deep within me, "Yes, of course. You. Hello." Now, a few years later, that seems ludicrous, preposterous—even to me. But not then. At that moment, it was far from strange.

Still, just as with so many of God's other remarkable responses to my prayers, I misunderstood the meaning of this one too. How obtuse I can be! What patience I require of God!

In this case, I latched onto our obedient, faithful, nearly unceasing prayers for Marc. It didn't seem coincidental to me that Marc's head was what my hand was in contact with when Christ made his remarkable appearance.

So I *wholeheartedly* believed that our prayer request (Marc's admission to West Point by Christmas) was being granted, and that this was God's way of telling me so.

I was wrong. Completely. Our prayer request wasn't granted by Christmas. In fact, it wasn't granted for five more months, five agonizing months, during which we all (Marc included) had to learn relinquishment.

When we finally were able to turn our prayer request back to God, when we no longer expected or demanded that it be fulfilled, when we released our need to see Marc at West Point and said, in effect, "Thy will be done," and when we really—*really*—meant it (I'm convinced this is key!), the dearest desire of Marc's heart was granted.

Just like that, God's "miracles" promise came true.

On May 1, 1986, a weekend after relinquishment of his dream, Marc received an invitation to become a member of the United States Military Academy's class of 1990.

He is, as I write this, well on his way toward graduation from West Point, a handsome cadet (so says a mother!) who is proud to be a member of "The Long Gray Line," who is a firm upholder of his sworn "Duty, Honor, Country" commitment, and who never questions how he got where he is or under whose Authority his West Point appointment finally arrived.

So why pray without ceasing if we have to relinquish our prayer requests?

All I can speak to is my own experience. I learned about God's faithfulness when I made the effort to be faithful to my Creator.

I learned about God's love when I absorbed *myself* in praise and adoration of the One who first loved me.

But perhaps most important of all, I learned the identity of my sons' True Parent. I learned how to place my children into God's care.

Knowing God

I love my children with everything in me, to the highest, deepest, most all-encompassing limits of my capacity. But my capacity to love doesn't cover even a corner of God's capacity.

I pray for my children's Christian walk, for their deepening faith, for their awareness of God at work in their lives.

I know my prayers will be answered. But through the years I've learned that I don't need to know in detail exactly how. I don't need to know in detail the methods God will use nor do I need to be privy to his timeline.

Ultimately, it is God's responsibility to bring our children into his kingdom.

Both of my children had their initial personal encounters with God in wholly different ways.

Marc's quest to know God began independently of us after a hit-and-run driver slammed into him while he rode his bike on our street after supper one evening. Kyle's began on a splendid star-filled night when a group of camp counselors re-enacted the story of Peter fleeing in fear from his denial of Christ.

Both boys sensed an outpouring of love focused directly on them. While they knew it came from somewhere, they knew it wasn't from us. Fred and I were physically absent during these life-altering moments.

Yet Marc and Kyle, alone but for God, were bathed in love. As only he can, the Lord of the universe brought each of my sons closer to the divine mystery and by doing so, created an insatiable hunger within them to learn more and yet more about him.

In neither case were Fred and I directly involved. Our role was important, but it was also indirect, tangential.

Our responsibility as parents is to develop hearts that care, that love, that already see the world through eyes similar to Christ's so that when Christ chooses to make himself known, our children can recognize him.

Nathaniel is a young child who lives hundreds and hundreds of miles away from grandparents, aunts and uncles, cousins. To help him keep in touch with family—to give him a sense of family—Nathaniel's parents have developed a unique prayer file.

The prayer file is a recipe box filled with index cards. On each card is a photograph of someone in Nathaniel's extended family. Every night before bedtime, one of the cards is pulled out. The person pictured on the card is the focus of Nathaniel's and his parents' prayers.

These wise and loving parents are preparing Nathaniel to meet his relatives, to help him feel at home with them when he sees them, to help him feel as if he already knows them well.

Isn't that our task as Christian parents? Aren't we preparing our children to meet Jesus so that when they see him for themselves, when they encounter Christ personally, they will recognize him and feel right at home?

But familiarity with Christ isn't static. We have a marvelous opportunity to help our children see what *we're* learning as Christians. We should be open and honest, allowing them to see how our relationship with God grows and changes. We can share our questions, our prayers.

Just as sincere questions bring powerful answers, so do sincere prayers. Through prayer, I've learned a new and liberating trust in God. I've learned that God holds my children's futures. I've learned that God has their best interests at heart.

Always.

I've also learned that God wants my children to grow in him and that he is much more aware than I am how to make that happen.

I've learned that what is most important is that my Lord and I stay in daily communion, that we regularly talk, that he knows *I* know the needs of my heart (in truth, *he* is the need of my heart), that I willingly and joyously seek him out, that I acknowledge each day I live that he is my Wonderful Counselor, my Prince of Peace, my Everlasting God.

I've learned that the biblical command to pray unceasingly is for *me*, not my kids. Except—and oh, this is so important!—it serves as a model for my kids to follow.

They know, because they've lived it, Who their parents' Source of Strength is.

Fred's and my prayer log is our children's future inheritance.

Whatever we leave in the way of material goods pales to immateriality in the face of this, the record of God's working in their lives while we, their earthly parents, faithfully prayed to their Heavenly Parent.

That, my friends, is the wonderful legacy of unceasing prayer. It's a legacy each of us can leave.

Questions for each of us to ask ourselves:
　　—What role does prayer play in my life, particularly in my life as a parent?
　　—How can I help my child develop a proper concept of God?
　　—Do I present a compartmentalized approach to Christianity? How can I avoid this pitfall?

A FINAL WORD

Parenting may happen automatically from a biological point of view, but it doesn't happen automatically once our children actually arrive, squalling and wondrous in their flesh-and-blood reality. Then we have to grit our teeth, dig in our heels, and begin working at being actively responsible for another human being.

No matter how much we learn about accomplishing this awesome task, there will always be more to learn. Our need to open ourselves to new insights and perspectives is constant.

Sometimes we must readjust our way of thinking about what it takes to be a good parent. And sometimes we must recognize and accept that the job will overwhelm us.

Count on it, we will commit some colossal blunders. But, through the grace of God, those blunders won't be fatal to our children.

It is important that our children recognize we are human. Only then are they freed to be human too.

When we make mistakes and learn from them, we set a healthy example. When we stumble and right ourselves and resolutely set off on a straighter course, we model a big part of what it means to be a child of God; we model being a learner.

If the teaching that fills our homes routinely emphasizes character development—routinely builds confidence, self-discipline, leadership, and faith into our children—can we trust that eventually they will rise above life's blows?

Without question.

Will those blows happen anyway?

Without question.

We parents are not in the business of disaster prevention, only in forearming for disaster survival.

There is a difference.

We are helpless to alter the events of our children's future, but we are not helpless to alter the environment of their present—which, in turn, provides them power to meet the future.

When we prepare our children to make a lifetime of choices, we make some choices of our own. Among them is how to build family fences.

Well, an Architect has left plans. But he requires you and me to be the carpenters, the stonemasons, the journeymen and women. He puts the trowel into our hands.

Family fences must be strong but they needn't be unblemished. Some of the mortar can seep out between the edges of a brick or two.

In the same way, children don't need *us* to be unblemished. In fact, it's destructive (not to mention downright dumb) for us to set parental perfection as a goal.

Why should we hope children will see an image of us that isn't there, that can never be there?

Even the best of us will remain human until our dying day. It's futile to pretend otherwise; inevitably, our children will find us out and despise us as phonies.

Children don't need to see that "advanced age" has somehow perfected us. They need to see how each of us, human beings all, learn to cope with life on planet earth.

Children must relate to us enough, must identify with our inner struggles enough, *not* to see how we make sense of life's certainties. Rather, they must see how we make sense of life's *un*certainties.

If Mom or Dad or some other human teacher, an adult they like and respect, can come to terms with frailty, then maybe they can too.

Court this task with hope and delight, and may God go with you as you do. May he bless and strengthen you, may he guide your steps and light your path.

That, by the way, isn't a benediction. It's an invocation.